Paul Hutchens

MOODY PRESS
CHICAGO

Revised Edition, 1998

Original Title: *Sugar Creek Gang Goes Western*

ISBN: 0-8024-7026-2

1 3 5 7 9 10 8 6 4 2

Printed in the United States of America

PREFACE

Hi—from a member of the Sugar Creek Gang!

It's just that I don't know which one I am. When I was good, I was Little Jim. When I did bad things—well, sometimes I was Bill Collins or even mischievous Poetry.

You see, I am the daughter of Paul Hutchens, and I spent many an hour listening to him read his manuscript as far as he had written it that particular day. I went along to the north woods of Minnesota, to Colorado, and to the various other places he would go to find something different for the Gang to do.

Now the years have passed—more than fifty, actually. My father is in heaven, but the Gang goes on. All thirty-six books are still in print and now are being updated for today's readers with input from my five children, who also span the decades from the '50s to the '70s.

The real Sugar Creek is in Indiana, and my father and his six brothers were the original Gang. But the idea of the books and their ministry were and are the Lord's. It is He who keeps the Gang going.

PAULINE HUTCHENS WILSON

1

We were in the middle of the most exciting part of a pretend cowboys' necktie party when we heard the shot.

It was one of the loudest shotgun blasts I had ever heard, and its echoes were like four or five fast thunders bounding through the Sugar Creek hills.

What on earth! I thought.

We all stood still and stared at each other with startled faces. We had been running in one direction and looking back in the opposite direction toward the old scarecrow that we had used for our bad man in our game of cowboys' necktie party.

We had strung up the scarecrow by his neck, hanging him from the branch of a river birch about twenty yards from the sandy beach of our swimming hole.

The ridiculous-looking old dummy we had named Snatzerpazooka was just where we wanted him now, at the edge of Dragonfly's father's cornfield. Hanging there in plain sight, swaying in the breeze, he would scare away the crows that had been digging up the new corn sprouts. Dragonfly, as you maybe know, was the nickname we had given to the pop-eyed member of the gang, whose actual name was Roy Gilbert.

The very minute Snatzerpazooka was up and swinging, we started on a helter-skelter run along the creek toward the spring. Following what we knew to be the pattern of cowboys in the Old West after a lynching, which they called a "necktie party," we were all galloping away on our imaginary horses, looking back and shooting with our voices, using our plastic and metal and wooden toy guns, yelling, *"Bang . . . bang . . . bang . . . bang-bang-bang!"*

I was seeing Snatzerpazooka over my shoulder, his ragged blue-and-white-striped overalls, his tied-on black hat, his crossbar. At the same time, I was galloping on my imaginary white stallion behind barrel-shaped Poetry, who was riding his own imaginary ordinary-looking roan horse.

The early summer wind was blowing in my hot face, my sleeves were flapping, and it felt good to be alive in a wonderful boys' world.

The rest of the gang were on their own different colored imaginary horses, yelling, *"Bang! Bang! Bang!"* as I was. All of us were emptying our imaginary six-shooters at the grotesque scarecrow dangling by his neck in the afternoon sun.

Right in the middle of our excitement was when we heard the *actual* shot from somebody's actual gun! It was an explosive blast that sent a shower of shivers all over me and scared me half to death.

As I've already told you, we all stopped and stared at each other, but not for long. Big Jim, our leader, barked, "Quick! Down! Drop flat—all of you!"

By *all* of us, he meant not only mischievous-minded, squawky-voiced Poetry; spindle-legged, pop-eyed Dragonfly; and red-haired, fiery-tempered, freckle-faced me, Bill Collins, son of Theodore Collins; but also Circus, our acrobat, and Little Jim, the littlest one of us and the best Christian.

In case you might be wondering why Little Tom Till wasn't with us on our necktie party, maybe I'd better tell you that all that spring and early summer, he had been chumming around with a new boy who had moved into the neighborhood. That new boy was our enemy—and it wasn't our fault, either. It hadn't felt good to lose Tom out of the gang—even though he wasn't exactly a member but only played with us and got to go with us on different camping trips.

Well, when Big Jim barked that fierce order for us to "drop flat," we obeyed like six boy-shaped lumps of lead—all of us except Poetry, who could only drop *round.*

Who, I wondered, had fired an actual gun? A *shotgun!*

We lay as quiet as six scared mice, straining our eyes to see through the sedge and ragweed and wild rosebushes and other growth, listening for all we were worth, and wondering, and worrying a little.

It certainly was a tense time. I could hear my heart beating, also the rippling riffle in the creek several feet behind me. Farther up the creek in the direction of our just-hung Snatzerpazooka, a saw-voiced crow was signaling with a rasping *"Caw! Caw!"* to his crow friends to stay away from the cornfield because there was a man around with a shotgun.

The smell of sweet clover from across the creek mingled with the odor of gun smoke.

Just then Dragonfly said wheezily, "*Look!* Snatzerpazooka's gone! He's down! His rope's broke!"

"He can't be!" I answered. "That was a leftover piece of Mom's clothesline, and that old scarecrow wasn't heavy enough to break it!"

A second later, though, my straining eyes told me Dragonfly was right. Even as far away as we were, I could see about five feet of rope dangling from the birch branch, and there wasn't any scarecrow hanging by his neck on the end of it.

"Maybe the knot came untied," Circus suggested.

Big Jim, beside and a little behind me, was peering over the top of a pile of drift left early that spring when Sugar Creek had overflowed its banks. He answered Circus, saying, "It couldn't have. I used a bowline knot, and that kind can't slip or jam!"

"It might have slipped off over his head," Circus growled back, maybe not wanting his idea squelched.

"If it had," Big Jim said deep in his throat, "the noose would still be there on the end of the rope"—which made good sense, because there was only the five feet of rope dangling in the breeze and no noose at the end.

Who, I worried, *had shot the shot and why? And where was our scarecrow?*

How long we all lay there whispering and wondering and trying to imagine who had shot the shot and why and what at, I don't know, but it seemed too long before Big Jim would let us get up and follow him back to the river birch to look around.

While you are imagining us crouching and half crawling our way along the edge of the cornfield that bordered the creek, like scouts scouting an enemy camp, wondering with us who had shot the shot and why and what or who at, I'd better also explain what a cowboys' necktie party is and why we had given our scarecrow such a name.

It was Dragonfly himself who had named him. Why he named him that was because of the strangest story you ever heard, the *oddest* thing that ever happened around Sugar Creek or maybe anyplace in the whole world.

You see, when Dragonfly was just a little guy, only about three-and-a-half years old—before there *was* any Sugar Creek Gang—he had no sisters or brothers and was lonesome most of the time. So he created a playmate out of his own imagination.

I never will forget the first time I heard the name *Snatzerpazooka* and how excited little Dragonfly was, how he yelled and cried, in fact actually *screamed,* when he thought his imaginary playmate wasn't going to get to go along with him and his folks when they went to town. It happened like this:

Dragonfly's parents with their little spindle-legged pop-eyed son, had stopped their car in front of our house beside the mailbox that has "Theodore Collins," my father's name, on it. While Mom and Dad stood in the shade of the walnut tree and visited with them through the car window, Dragonfly and I monkeyed around the iron pitcher pump, which is not far from our back door.

Feeling mischievous at the time, I thrust my hand into the stream of water Dragonfly was pumping into the iron kettle there, and, just as quick, flicked some of the water into his face.

A second later, he started to gasp and to wrinkle up his nose and the rest of his face. He looked toward the sun and let out a long-tailed sneeze, then said, "Snatzerpazooka!"

"Stop that! Don't sneeze like that!" he cried.

"I didn't sneeze," I answered him. "You did!"

"I did not!" he argued back. "*He* did!"

"He *who* did?" I asked.

That's when he used the word in his normal voice, saying, "Snatzerpazooka did!"

I looked at his dragonflylike eyes, which had a strange expression in them. "Who in the world is Snatzerpazooka?" I exclaimed. I was pumping a tin of water at the time. I tossed the water over the iron kettle into the puddle on the ground there, scaring a flock of yellow and white butterflies out of their butterfly wits and scattering them in about seventeen different directions.

Dragonfly started to answer, got a mussed-up expression on his face, and let out another noisy, explosive sneeze with Snatzerpazooka mixed up in it.

His father called then from the car, saying, "Hurry up, Roy! We have to get there before two o'clock!"

"Just a minute!" Dragonfly yelled toward his father. Then he did the weirdest thing. He looked around in a circle and swung into a fast run out across the grassy yard, dodging this way and that like a boy trying to catch a young rooster his folks are going to have for dinner.

"Stop, you little rascal!" Dragonfly kept yelling. "Stop, or I'll leave you here!"

Then Dragonfly's father's deep voice thundered over Mom and Dad's heads toward his zigzagging son, now near the plum tree. "Roy! Stop running around like a chicken with its head off, or we'll drive on without you!"

Dragonfly stopped, and a minute later he was on his way to the gate. He was a little slow getting through it—*over* it, rather, because he was trying to do what Dad had ordered me never to do. He was climbing up the gate's cross wires to climb *over* the gate, when all he would have had to do would have been to lift the latch and walk through.

The minute Dragonfly was on the ground, he reached back and up with both arms, as if he was reaching for something or somebody, and I heard him say scoldingly, "Come on! Jump! I'll catch you!"

"Roy Gilbert!" Dragonfly's father growled again gruffly. "Hurry up!"

"I can't," Dragonfly whined back. "I can't get him to get off the gate! He's stubborn and won't do what I tell him!" Dragonfly kept on not hurrying and not getting into the car's open backdoor, which I could see his impatient father was wanting him to hurry up and do.

A second later Mr. Gilbert's temper came to life, and he was out of the front seat in a hurry. He scooped up his son in his strong arms, carried him struggling to the car, half-tossed him into the backseat, slammed the door after him, and quickly got into the front seat again beside Dragonfly's worried-faced mother.

The car engine ground itself into noisy life. In a minute the Gilbert family would go speeding down the road, stirring up a cloud of white dust that would ride on the afternoon breeze across the field toward Strawberry Hill.

That's when Dragonfly let out a yell with tears in it, crying, "Wait! Don't go yet! He's still back there on the gate!"

Next, that little rascal shoved open the car door, swung himself out, scooted to the fence, helped his imaginary playmate off onto the ground, shoved him into the backseat, and climbed in after him.

What, I thought, *on earth!*

As soon as the Gilberts' car was gone and

the lazy cloud of dust was already on its way across the field, I heard Mom say to Dad, "At least our boy isn't as bad as *that!* Whatever is wrong with Roy, anyway?"

"Nothing's wrong with him," Dad answered. "He's just a normal boy who needs a little brother or sister to play with. Not having any, he has created one out of his own lively imagination."

Hearing Mom and Dad say that to each other while they were still on the other side of the gate, I broke in with a mischievous grin in my voice, saying, "*I* don't have any brothers or sisters, either."

That was before my little sister, Charlotte Ann, was born, which you know all about if you've read the very first Sugar Creek Gang story there ever was—the one that is called *The Swamp Robber.*

I had my right foot on one of the cross wires of the gate as if I was going to climb up and over.

Dad gave me a half-savage stare through the woven wire and, with a set jaw, exclaimed an order to me, which was, "Don't you *dare!* And we have enough trouble keeping *you* out of mischief! What would we do with *another* one of you?"

For some reason my foot slipped off the cross wire, and I was quickly off to the big rope swing under the walnut tree to pump myself into a high back-and-forth swing. I was wishing at the same time that I *did* have a little brother to play with. I was also wondering what if I made for myself an imaginary playmate? What would he look like, and what would I name him? What a crazy name—Snatzerpazooka!

And what a lot of crazy experiences we had that summer with Dragonfly himself.

Dragonfly's parents worried about their boy for a while—what with his all the time talking to his ridiculous playmate, acting all the time as if there were two of him, having fights and arguments with a person nobody except Dragonfly could see or hear. That boy certainly had a "vivid imagination," Mom said one day.

In fact, his parents got to worrying about him so much that they took him to a doctor in the city, a special kind of doctor who understood children's minds. They found out it was almost the same as what Dad had already told Mom.

"There's nothing wrong with him that having a pet or a real-life playmate won't cure. Snatzerpazooka will just fade out of the picture after your boy starts to school or when he begins normal boy-life activities," the doctor told them.

But Snatzerpazooka didn't fade out. Dragonfly was so used to him and had so much fun playing with his imaginary playmate that even after he began going to school, and after the Sugar Creek Gang was started, he still hung onto him.

Many a time when we were down along the creek somewhere or up at the abandoned cemetery having a gang meeting and something important was brought to a vote, Dragonfly would make us let Snatzerpazooka vote, too.

Poetry worked harder than the rest of us trying to help Dragonfly forget his imaginary playmate. He refused to call him Snatzerpazooka but gave him the name Shadow instead. The two had an honest-to-goodness fight about it one day down at the spring. We had all finished getting down on our knees and drinking out of the reservoir the way cows do—that is, all of us had our drink except Dragonfly.

He stood back near the board fence, waiting till we were through. Poetry, being in a mischievous mood, and still on his hands and knees at the reservoir, looked back toward Dragonfly and said, "Here, Shadow, come get your drink!" He then went through the motions of helping Dragonfly's imaginary playmate onto *his* hands and knees, bent his head forward and down to the surface of the water, saying, "You're a pretty dumb little bunny. Don't you know how to drink like a cow? You *look* like one! Get your head *down!*"

Then Poetry gave Shadow's imaginary head a shove clear down under the water, his own right hand going under with it.

In seconds, Dragonfly was like a young tiger. He leaped forward and down onto Poetry's back and started whamming him with both fists, demanding, "You stop dunking him!"

Poetry stopped all right. He was bowled over by Dragonfly's flying attack and a split second later was on his stomach in the almost icy water. He came up sputtering and spitting water. Reaching behind him, he caught Snatzerpazooka's *live* playmate by both his slender arms and ducked *his* head under as far as he had Snatzerpazooka's imaginary head.

Big Jim came to the rescue of both of them by stopping the fight and saying, "Come on, Snatzerpazooka! You come on up into the sunlight with me and get dried out. You'll catch your death of cold." With that he went through the motions of picking up the imaginary little boy and carrying him up the incline. Dragonfly himself hurried along after them.

By the time I got there, our spindle-legged pal was as far as the stump we later named the Black Widow Stump and on his way toward home. He had his right hand out behind him as though he was leading somebody, and I heard him say, "Come on, pal! Those roughnecks don't know how to treat a gentleman!"

No sooner had Dragonfly and his just-dunked imaginary playmate disappeared over the rim of the hill than Poetry started quoting one of the many poems he had memorized. It was one most of us knew by heart ourselves. It was by Robert Louis Stevenson, and in Poetry's squawky, ducklike voice it sounded almost funny:

"I have a little shadow that goes in and
out with me,
And what can be the use of him is
more than I can see.

He is so very, very like me from the
heels up to the head,
And I see him jump before me, when I
jump into my bed."

Poetry was yelling the poem as loud as he could, so that Dragonfly could hear it. He started on the second verse but got interrupted by Dragonfly sneezing in a long-tailed, extraloud voice and exclaiming, "Snatzerpazooka!"

Poetry yelled back a mimicking sneeze and cried, "Snatzerpa*shadow!*"

Because we all liked Dragonfly a lot, we decided at a special meeting to pretend along with him, letting him take Snatzerpazooka along with us whenever he wanted to, waiting for the imaginary little rascal when we had to, helping him over the fences, even carrying him when Dragonfly said he was too tired to walk.

Dragonfly didn't cause us much trouble that first summer. The only thing was, Snatzerpazooka began to change a little. From being a helpless, innocent little fellow that had to be carried or helped over fences, he began to get ornery. Sometimes we'd hear Dragonfly quarreling with him and calling him names.

One summer day when I was down along the bayou not far from the Black Widow Stump, I felt a sneeze coming on. I twisted my face into a Dragonflylike tailspin and burst out with an explosive "Snatzerpazooka!" loud enough to be heard all the way to the clump of evergreens at the edge of the bayou.

Poetry was with me at the time, and being in a mischievous mood he mimicked me with a sneeze just like mine, which in his squawky voice sounded like a guinea hen with a bad cold. His sneeze, in the middle of which he cried, "Snatzerpashadow!" instead of "Snatzerpazooka!" hadn't any sooner exploded out across the bayou than there was a saucy yell from behind the evergreens crying, "You stop that! There isn't any Snatzerpazooka!"

Then, from behind those evergreens shot a spindle-legged, pop-eyed boy. A brown-and-tan puppy with a crank-handle tail leaped along beside him.

That was when we found out there wasn't any Snatzerpazooka anymore—or wasn't supposed to be, anyway.

Dragonfly was both mad and glad: mad at us for sneezing the way we had, and happy all over because his parents had gotten him a dog playmate. He told us how much the dog cost and what a good trailer he was.

"Looks like a bloodhound," Poetry said. "Here, Red, come here and let me cheer you up a little!"

He was one of the saddest-faced dogs I'd ever seen. His hair was smooth but seemed very loose, as if he had three times as much as he needed, or as if his mother had made him a hair coat that was a lot too big for him. His skin was extrawrinkled on the forehead, and his ears were long and floppy.

"He *is* a bloodhound," Dragonfly boasted.

"He's half bloodhound and half beagle. That's how come it was so easy to find you guys. I put him on your trail, and he led me straight to you. See here?"

Dragonfly held out to me my old straw hat, which that very morning I'd been wearing around the house and barn and had left on the ground under the plum tree.

"How come he didn't bawl on the trail?" Poetry asked.

We'd all hunted at night with Circus's dad's hounds, and when they were trailing, there was plenty of dog noise.

Dragonfly's proud answer was "He's going to be a *still* trailer."

That was hard to believe, yet there was my old straw hat, and here was Dragonfly with his hound pup, which right that minute was sniffing at me and wagging his crank-handle tail as much as to say, "Here's your criminal! He smells just like his hat! Now what do you want me to do?"

You never saw such a happy little guy as Dragonfly over his droopy-faced hound. The doctor had been right. Dragonfly needed a real-life playmate—a human being or a pet, he had said.

"How do you like that?" Poetry said to me one day a little later. "Having us for playmates wasn't enough. He had to have a floppy-eared, droopy-faced, crank-tailed, loose-skinned half bloodhound!"

Dad explained it this way: "He could be with you boys only part of the time. He needed a playmate *all* the time for a while—at home as well as at school and at play. He'll be all right from now on. You just wait and see."

We *did* wait and see. But Dad was wrong, as wrong as he had ever been in his life. Just *how* wrong, I'll tell you in the next chapter.

2

For quite a while we didn't hear any more of Snatzerpazooka, Dragonfly's ornery little shadow, except for when one of us would sneeze. Now and then we'd cry out the way Dragonfly used to do, exclaiming, "Snatzerpa-zooka!" just for fun.

We stopped doing even that when we woke up to the fact that it really hurt the little guy to be teased about what a dumb bunny he used to be.

"Snatzerpazooka's dead!" he told Poetry and me one day. "He died yesterday, and Red-skin and I buried him down by the mouth of the cave." Redskin was the name Dragonfly had finally settled on for his hound.

Poetry looked at me and I at him, and he said under his breath, "He's still imagining things!"

"I am not!" Dragonfly, who heard him, exclaimed. "Come on, and I'll show you!"

He did show us. Under the hollow sycamore tree just off the path that leads into the swamp, there was a small oblong mound of new earth, the kind you see in cemeteries after somebody has just been buried. Erected at one end was a slab of wood and on it some crudely lettered words:

SNATZERPAZOOKA GILBERT
Horse Thief. Died by Hanging.

There wasn't room on the slab for any other words. I stood looking down at the grave and at the marker, and there was the strangest feeling in my heart. It almost seemed maybe a real person was buried there. A lump came into my throat and almost choked me. I could hardly see the grave or the marker for the tears that all of a sudden were in my eyes.

I looked into Dragonfly's own red-rimmed eyes, and there were tears there too. He swallowed hard a few times and sniffled a little. Also, I saw his face start into its usual tailspin and look as wrinkled on the forehead as his dog's, and I knew he was going to sneeze.

That was when I learned for sure that in Dragonfly's mind his imaginary playmate was really dead, because his long-tailed sneeze came out like anybody's ordinary *"Ker-choo!"*

That summer passed, and the mound of earth settled until it was level with the other soil around it. Autumn leaves fell on it, and winter snow covered it. The only thing left was the wooden marker. Then one day when the gang was trying to start a fire at the mouth of the cave, Dragonfly brought the marker from the grave and, with his Scout hatchet, split it into kindling wood, and we burned it.

And that was the end of Snatzerpazooka until the summer this story started.

A lot of other things started that summer,

too. One of them was a lot of new trouble the gang had with a boy who had moved into the neighborhood. You've probably read about him in some of the other Sugar Creek stories. But just in case you haven't, his name was Shorty Long. I'd had my very first rough-and-tumble fight with him on a snowy day in the book called *Palm Tree Manhunt* and the last one in the summer in *The Blue Cow.*

Shorty Long was one of the fiercest fighters I had ever had to lick. He was also the worst one that had ever licked me a few times.

Shorty was the kind of boy who liked to have a playmate he could boss around, or he wasn't happy. Dragonfly had been his first choice, and he had ruled that allergic-nosed little guy like a wicked king ruling a slave. For a while we almost lost Dragonfly in the blue cow story, because at first Dragonfly *liked* Shorty Long and enjoyed being ordered around by him.

Dragonfly was the kind of boy that had to have a close friend, too. Maybe that was the reason he had used his imagination to create his make-believe playmate, Snatzerpazooka.

As soon as Dragonfly was free from the bully, though, he had come back to us, and the gang was happy again. All of us got together as often as we could.

Shorty Long's folks went away nearly every winter to Florida or to some other warm place, so it was mostly in the summer that he was our biggest problem.

The only other boys that had caused the gang trouble were Bob and Tom Till, who lived across the creek. Bob was also the bully type of boy and was always lording it over his red-haired, freckle-faced little brother.

Tom, as you may remember, was *almost* a member of the gang and played with us a lot. Their father, old hook-nosed John Till, was one of the worst men in the county and spent about half his time in jail and the other half out. He never took the boys to Sunday school or to church, which was maybe one reason his boys were like ragweed instead of sweet clover.

Well, the summer this story started, Shorty Long was just back with his folks from Arizona where they'd spent the winter. Right away Shorty picked out a boy in the neighborhood to chum around with. Not being able to rule any of the gang, he managed to get Tom Till instead.

Tom was a poor boy and did not have much money to spend, and Shorty's folks were rich enough to go to a warm climate every winter, so Shorty bribed Tom by giving him spending money for things Tom couldn't afford—things such as a new Scout knife, a pair of field glasses, even a cook kit with aluminum utensils. All the parts of the cook kit nested and locked together and didn't rattle when you carried them in their khaki carrying case.

Also, they pitched Shorty's tent on the other side of the creek, down below the Sugar Creek bridge under the tall cottonwood. It was straight across from the mouth of the branch on our side.

It didn't feel good to see the two of them chumming around together along the creek and the bayou, playing they were pirates, building their campfires, and cooking their dinner over the open fire the same as we did. After we'd given each other a licking in the Battle of Bumblebee Hill, Tom had been one of my best friends and had been coming to Sunday school with us once in a while. It hurt me to realize that he was being a pal with a boy who was as ornery to the gang as he could be.

Many a time that early summer, we'd stand on the bridge and look downstream to the khaki tent under the cottonwood and see the smoke rising from their campfire, hear their laughing, and feel hurt in our hearts that we'd lost Tom. He was avoiding us now, even when he was by himself and Shorty Long was nowhere around.

I never will forget the time Mom sent me over to the Tills' house to take a cake she had baked for Tom's mother's birthday and to invite Tom to go to Sunday school with our family the next morning. That was the day I got insulted. Also it was a very important day for another reason.

Tom stood on their back porch and looked at me as if I was just so much dirt. With a sneer in his voice he said, "Sissies go to Sunday school!"

Well, *that* fired me up. If his mother hadn't

been just inside the kitchen door talking to my mom on the phone to thank her for the cake, I'd have let my two hard-knuckled fists and my muscled arms prove to him that there was one boy who went to Sunday school who wasn't a sissy.

I didn't sock him with my fists, though. But I did with my thoughts and also with several words from my mind, a piece of which I hurled at him as hard as I did a fastball when I was pitching in a baseball game. Maybe I'd better tell you what I said, though I shouldn't have, because it was like a boomerang that the native people of Australia use, which comes back when they throw it and sometimes hits them on the head if they don't dodge.

What I yelled to Little Tom Till that day, as he stood on the porch of his house glaring sullenly at me, was, "The very next time I catch you alone somewhere without Shorty or your brother along, I'm going to whale the living daylights out of you!"

Just saying it stirred my temper up that much worse, and I was almost blind with anger. I could even see the place on his jaw where I wished I could land a fierce fast fist.

Instead, though, I gritted my teeth, felt the muscles of my jaw tighten, and just glared back at him.

To make me madder, he swung around to the long-handled, wooden pump behind him and said, "Maybe a little water will cool you off!" With that he took several fast strokes, pumped a tin full, and slammed it into my face.

Now what do you do at a time like that?

You probably *feel* just like I did. First, you feel the shock of the cold water striking you in your hot face, because you are already extra-hot from having pedaled all the way over on your bicycle. Then you feel a surge of temper racing in your veins. Everything sort of whirls in your mind like a windmill in a storm. Then you go blind with rage, and you're not a sissy anymore but a mad bull ready to charge head-first into the cause of your trouble.

That was what I felt like, and what I'd started to do, when from behind me I heard somebody's gruff voice saying grimly, "I wouldn't do it, Bill. You *are* all wet, you know. He was just trying to help you realize it."

I whirled—and it was Shorty Long himself, standing just outside the Tills' picket gate, his jaw set, his squinting eyes focused on me, his lips pursed, and in his hands a baseball bat.

Then I knew why Tom had been so brave and so ornery with me. Shorty Long, with whom he'd been palling around and for whom he was like Robinson Crusoe's man Friday, had poisoned his mind against us and against any boy who was trying to live up to what he learned in Sunday school and church.

I stood and stared—maybe *glared*—at Shorty a minute, trying to hold myself back from charging headfirst into a baseball bat.

The sermon I'd heard several weeks before

seemed to be standing between me and a bashed nose. Even as I stood with my back to Tom Till, wiping the water off my face and facing my enemy, the Bible verse that had been our minister's text went galloping around in my mind. It was as if Somebody with a very kind, strong voice was saying, "He who is slow to anger is better than the mighty, and he who rules his spirit, than he who captures a city."

That had been one of the best sermons I'd ever heard. I had been sitting by the open east window in our church at the time, listening to the sermon and also to the birds outside in the trees. It seemed maybe our minister had picked out that special Bible verse because it fit me like a new pair of jeans.

"Every Christian has two natures," he said and explained that it was up to us to decide which nature was the boss—the good or the bad.

It seemed that Dragonfly wasn't the only one who had a playmate. I, too, had one, and he wasn't imaginary, either. And mine certainly wasn't dead and buried in a hole in the ground beside the sycamore tree but was alive and lived inside me.

One other thing our minister had said, and which I would probably never forget, was, "If you're having trouble ruling your spirit, try praying about it."

Those words came back to me right that minute while I was standing inside Tom Till's picket fence, frowning at Shorty Long and his savage-looking baseball bat.

Shorty kept on scowling at me. His brows were down and his lips pursed, his hands gripping the bat handle.

I kept on standing, fighting the Snatzerpazooka that was inside me, which was trying to make me make a fighting fool out of myself.

Shorty Long's sarcastic voice broke into my stormy thoughts right then, saying, "Your bike is right here, if you're scared and want to run away." He stepped back and swung the gate open for me to get through.

Tom's mother came out then with the empty cake pan, and, because it seemed there wasn't anything else that I ought to do, I thanked her for the pan. I told her I hoped she had a happy birthday and a little later, with gritted teeth, was on my bike pedaling down the narrow, dusty footpath through their orchard to their other gate by the barn.

I certainly felt strange inside. I hadn't gotten into any actual fight, but I hadn't ruled my spirit, either. Shorty Long's baseball bat had ruled it for me.

I was still boiling inside as I pedaled furiously along the gravel road toward the bridge on my way home. The faster I pumped, the worse I felt and the more angry I was at Shorty Long for doing what he was doing to Tom Till.

When I reached the bridge, I slowed down, then stopped and looked downstream toward the tall cottonwood and caught a glimpse of the roof of the brown tent.

That is when my spirit started to rule *me.*

It told me to leave my bike leaning against the bridge railing, run back, pick up some stones from the gravel road, and see if I could throw as straight and as far with them as I could with a baseball; see if, maybe, I could hit the slanting canvas roof of Shorty Long's tent.

It took only a few minutes to get back to my bike with several stones.

I decided to look first toward Tom Till's house to see if a big boy with a baseball bat in his hands was looking this way. Of course, I knew Shorty Long couldn't run fast enough to get to me for at least five minutes, but . . . well, what I was about to do . . . if I did it . . . which it seemed like I shouldn't . . . ought to be kept secret.

Just that second I heard a red-winged blackbird let loose with his very juicy-noted melody, which is one of the most cheerful songs a boy ever hears. In fact, it seemed there were two or three scarlet-shouldered singers singing several songs the same second, making it seem a wonderful world to live in. If there was anybody who was feeling disgusted with life, he ought to cheer up.

My arm was back, ready for the toss. I took a quick glance to the right where there was a marshy place with willows bordering it, and saw old Redwing himself perched on one of the top branches, swaying and letting out his whistling *"Oucher-la-ree-e!"* followed a few seconds later with another. Then, from the other side of the narrow, marshy place, another red-wing whistled the same thing.

That's when I heard the frogs piping, too—one of the other almost-most-beautiful sounds a boy ever hears.

That's also when I took my stubborn, angry spirit by the scruff of its neck and shook it the way one of Circus's dad's hounds shakes a rat. Then, with a whirl around in the opposite direction, I threw the stone as far upstream as I could, where it landed with a big splash right in the center of the creek.

I let out a heavy sigh and started to swing onto my bike to pedal across the bridge toward home, then took another look downstream toward the tent.

That is when I noticed a curl of smoke rising not far from the cottonwood.

Their campfire, I thought. *They'll maybe cook supper there and stay all night.*

It wasn't much of a fire, judging by the amount of smoke. Still, a boy ought not to go away and leave an open fire burning—*ever.* Our camp director, Barry Boyland, who had taken us on a few trips, had always made us put out our fires before we left camp. Always.

It had been a pretty dry spring too. There could be a bad brushfire if the blaze should begin to spread.

Enemy or no enemy, it seemed I ought to race down to the fire and put it out.

It took only a few minutes for me to get to the end of the bridge and down the embankment on the well-worn path made by barefoot boys' feet, running along the zigzagging trail that skirted the creek bank on my way to the fire.

"That's an awful lot of smoke now for a campfire," I said to myself as smoke got in my eyes, making it hard to see and making me cough. Even little Tom Till should have known better than to leave a live campfire. Tom had been with us on one of our trips into the wilds of the North, and he'd known all the camp rules for safety.

As I ran, my mind made up to put out the fire, I was seeing the scowling face of Shorty Long and the baseball bat in his hands. I was hearing him say, "Your bike is right here, if you're scared and want to run away!"

My footpath led all of a sudden into the opening where their tent was pitched. I let out a gasp when I saw what I saw—not a small patch of burned ground with a ring of ashes and a little campfire in the center, but a circle of fire about fifteen feet wide with leaping, excited flames all around the outside edges. The nervous, yellow fire-tongues were eating into the dried marsh grass left from last year's growth, and the fire was within only a few yards of the tent itself.

How, I asked myself, was I to put out such a fierce, fast flame? What with?

My eyes took in the whole area around the camp, and there wasn't a thing a boy could use to smother a fire.

Faster than a flock of pigeons zooming over

our barn, my thoughts flew back to the time the gang had once put out a fire that was running wild through an Indian cemetery in the North woods when we'd been on a camping trip up there. We'd done it by yanking off our shirts, dashing down a steep incline to the lake, getting our shirts soaking wet, and using them to flail the flames. We'd worked like a fire department to save the dozens of little Indian wooden grave markers, which actually were small houses, each one about the size of a Sugar Creek doghouse.

Maybe there would be a gunnysack inside the tent, I thought. I could use that and save the new plaid shirt I had on—in fact, had put on specially for the trip to take the cake to Tom Till's mother.

But the smoke was blowing toward the tent, and I couldn't see inside.

A wild idea came to me then. Quick untie the tent ropes and move the whole tent out of the way of the fire. But that'd be too hard a job for so little time.

There wasn't even an old shirt or pair of trousers hanging on any tree or bush as there sometimes is around a camp.

In my excitement, I kept thinking of that fierce, fast fire we'd fought up North and how easily we had put it out with our soaking-wet shirts. The red-and-green plaid I had on was one I liked better than any my folks had ever bought me. My oldish, well-worn blue jeans might be better for fighting fire, I thought.

But there wasn't any time to be lost if I wanted to save the tent and also stop what could quickly become a bad brushfire. There hadn't been any rain around Sugar Creek for quite a while, and everything was as dry as tinder.

It had to be pants or shirt, one or the other.

I started on the run for the creek and on the way decided it had to be the shirt. It would come off easier. Quicker than anything, I had it off and in another jiffy was racing with it, soaking wet, to the fire.

Save the tent, first! my very common sense told me.

Wham! Wham! Wham! . . . Squish! Squish! Squish! . . . Puff! Puff! Puff! . . . Pant! Pant! Pant! . . . Cough! Cough! Cough!

My blood raced in my veins, the wind blew smoke in my face, the heat was smothering.

In maybe seven minutes, which seemed like an hour, I had the whole fire out. I'd saved Shorty Long's tent and everything in it.

I didn't even take time to look and be proud of my work, because what if Shorty and Tom would all of a sudden come down to see what all the smoke had been about and would find me there? They'd think I had been the cause of the fire. They wouldn't even bother to wonder who had put it out, and there might be plenty of trouble. More than plenty.

Up the embankment I went like a shirtless chipmunk. In a few moments I had my sopping-wet, smudged shirt in the wire basket of my bike on top of the empty cake pan and was pedaling home.

I felt fine. I had ruled my spirit. I was better in the sight of the One who had made me than Julius Caesar when he had captured a city.

Beside the road in Poetry's dad's meadow, a meadowlark let loose with his very piercing song, which sounded like "spring of the year!" The meadowlark, I happened to think, was one of Mom's favorite birds. She liked the cardinal best.

Thinking of Mom reminded me of my wet, smoke-smudged shirt, and for some reason I slowed down a little in my fast pedaling toward home.

When I came to the corner where I would turn east, I stopped and read one or two horse posters tacked to the big sugar tree there. I always enjoyed looking at pictures of horses, liking them almost better than any other tame animal.

Catty-corner across the road in Poetry's dad's woods, which were being used for pasture that spring, was another big sugar tree with low-hanging branches. The ground all around its trunk was stomped free of grass. That was where Mr. Thompson's horses always stood on hot days to be in the shade, and where, when it rained, they went to keep from getting so wet. The overhanging branches reached out as far as fifteen feet all around the trunk.

I noticed their different-colored horses were scattered through the woods, their heads down, munching grass.

Quite a ways from the tree, I saw Poetry's pinto standing by himself, nibbling at the leaves of a red-haw bush. My heart leaped with happiness as I watched him for a minute, wishing I had one like him. He was different from any riding horse I'd ever seen. He was yellow and black and white, and his eyes were like crystal.

"In Texas," Poetry had told me, "they call ponies like Thunderball 'paint ponies.'"

Thunderball was certainly a fine name for him, because when you were riding him, you felt like wild thunder galloping across the sky. Tomorrow, maybe I'd get to take a ride on him all by myself, as Poetry had been letting me do several times a week ever since his folks bought Thunderball for him.

"Ho-hum," I yawned. I was still hot from the hard work of putting out the fire, and the day itself was very sultry for spring.

The sun was still pretty high, but the southeast sky had big yellowish-white clouds in it. They were piled cloud on cloud like a mountain, making the sky look the way it does sometimes in the middle of the summer before a thunderstorm.

Maybe I'd better get on home and help get the chores done, I thought.

There was a happy feeling inside me now as I pedaled up the gravel road between the woods on my left and our orchard on the right. I had ruled my spirit, and I was on my way to give Mom or Dad or both a chance to rule theirs when they saw what putting out a dangerous brushfire could do to a boy's new red and green plaid shirt.

It seemed, though, that the piles of yellowish-white clouds high in the south and east were talking to me, saying, "There's going to be a storm. There's going to be a storm!"

3

The nearer I came to Theodore Collins's mailbox, the more I wondered what Theodore Collins, in the barn doing the chores, would say about my shirt, and what *Mrs.* Theodore Collins, in the house getting supper, would say and *do* about it.

I had my speech all planned. I knew just what I would say when they asked me what had happened and why.

One or the other of them would find out about it first—or else they'd both notice it at the same time—and one or the other of them would say, "Bill Collins! What on earth happened to your shirt? What kind of an excuse can you give for completely ruining a brand-new shirt?"

I would rule my spirit and say calmly, as I washed up for supper, "I haven't any excuse, but if you'd be interested in a very good *reason,* I'll be pleased to give you one."

One or the other of them would then give me a kind of sharp answer, saying, "It'll take *seven* reasons to explain *that* shirt! Just *look* at it!" Mom herself would hold it up by the shoulders and exclaim at it with shaking head and crinkled face. "What on *earth!*"

I'd keep on ruling my spirit to show them

how easily it could be done and say offhandedly, "Oh, there was a little fire down along the creek that was about to grow into a very bad brushfire, and to keep it from burning up Shorty Long's tent, I decided to put it out."

That was the way I'd planned the conversation to go.

And that was the way it *didn't* go.

I got through the front gate and leaned my bike against the grape arbor post. Then, after wrapping the wet, smoke-smudged shirt in an old newspaper and laying it on the floor of the toolshed, I eased my way into the house without being noticed. I knew exactly where I'd left the well-worn blue shirt I'd taken off before changing to the new one, just before starting over to Tom Till's house with the cake.

I was on my way out the kitchen door with my old shirt on my back and my new one on my mind when I saw Mom come out of the barn with a basket of eggs. I met her halfway across the barnyard, just as Dad came out of the west stable door with a pail of milk.

Mixy, our old black-and-white cat, came out the stable door at the same time and ran all around Dad and the three-gallon milk pail, mewing up at him and making it hard for him to walk straight.

Just then a rumble of thunder broke into my thoughts, and I noticed the sky had almost twice as many clouds as it had had a little while before.

It might be a good idea to get my folks'

minds onto the weather, I thought, and yelled to Dad, "Looks like it's going to rain!"

He stopped, whirled around with the milk pail in his hand, and yelled down to Mixy, "Scat, cat! Give me a little time! Bill, you run and shut the barn doors, will you? I don't want that load of hay to get wet!"

The wind switched directions just then and started blowing hard from the west, and it looked for a few minutes as if the storm would strike before we could get the chores finished.

Mom, with her basket of eggs, took a worried look at the sky and exclaimed, "They're green! Green clouds mean hail!" There was excitement in her voice, and she started on a blue-skirted run toward the house, calling back, "I'll get the upstairs window!"

The whole Collins family flew into action—Dad getting to the house with the milk in spite of Mixy, I getting the east barn doors shut and bolted and yelling to a barnyard full of hens to hurry up and get into their own house before they got soaking wet, and Mom flying upstairs to get the south bedroom window closed.

What a storm! The sky was so dark that, when we all got inside the house, Mom turned on the lights in the kitchen and the living room. Then we settled down to a kind of scared wait, while the rain beat on the roof and against the windows. For a while it seemed there never had been so much thunder or so loud.

Charlotte Ann, who nearly always liked to

be on Dad's lap when we were in the house—when she wasn't pestering me for a piggyback ride or fussing for attention—made *Mom* hold her, burying her cute little face against Mom's breast whenever there was a blinding flash of lightning and a wild clap of thunder that shook the house.

There was a wild wind too, and we wondered if maybe there would be a tornado.

After a while, though, the thunder began to sound farther away, and the sky became lighter. A little later, when I looked out the east window, I saw a shaft of sunlight slanting across the cornfield. There were puddles of water everywhere and little rivulets running across the barnyard and in the ditches along the road.

"Look!" Mom exclaimed from the east window of the living room. "There's a *rainbow!*"

Then she quoted a verse from the Bible, which goes, *"I set My bow in the cloud."* I looked at Mom's face, and all the worry that had been on it was gone. It seemed she wasn't looking just at the rainbow with its beautiful colored arch hanging over the east, but at something a lot farther away. Maybe she was thinking about the One who gave the world the very first rainbow there ever was.

While Mom was in such a peaceful frame of mind, and after such a thundery storm, it seemed the wrong time to mention the soiled shirt.

My mind took a hop, skip, and a jump down to the Sugar Creek bridge and Shorty Long's tent, and I realized it might not have been necessary for me to put out that fire. The rain would have done it for me—only it might have been too late.

Neither Mom nor Pop seemed to remember I'd had on my new plaid shirt when I'd left for the Tills' house with the cake, and, of course, they hadn't seen me riding home in my bare skin and wondered how come.

Mom flew into getting supper. Dad and I went out into the cool, rainwashed air to wind up the rest of the chores. It was Saturday, and, as you probably know, the Collins family and nearly every other family in the whole Sugar Creek territory went to town on Saturday nights to buy groceries and to see who else had come to town. Mom always liked to see the different women who were on our party telephone line, in order to finish talking about different things they couldn't talk about on the phone and also to find out if there were any new babies born anywhere and what their names were.

On a street corner somewhere, Dad nearly always managed to find quite a few other husbands who were tired of waiting for their wives to finish shopping and talking, and in that way he would catch up with all the farm news in the country.

Saturday night was also a good night for the gang, because nearly always quite a few of us went to town, too, and we liked to eat caramel corn and peanuts and just walk round and round the main block of Main Street.

Supper was on the table and eaten in a hurry, and still nobody had even thought about my plaid shirt—nobody except me, that is.

"Hurry up, you two," Mom ordered us from the front bedroom where she was standing at the large dresser mirror finishing her face and hair. "Bill, you can wear your new plaid shirt, the one you wore over to Tills' to take the cake."

For a half second my mind's eye looked out across the Collins family sky, and it seemed the clouds were building up for a storm.

Dad, who right then was in the back bedroom changing his own clothes, called me to hurry and come in and change mine.

In a few worried minutes, I was in where Dad was. He was standing with his Saturday night pants on but with no shirt, looking into the wardrobe where about seven different colored, freshly laundered shirts were hanging in a row, all fresh from Mom's iron.

Selecting one just as I came in, he slipped it off the hanger and started to put it on. Then he stopped and inspected a tiny, very neatly stitched patch near the collar where the collar point had worn it through and Mom had fixed it.

"Come here, son. Let me show you something," he ordered.

I came, looking at the row of shirts and being reminded again that my own shirt was wrapped in a newspaper out in the toolshed. I was seeing it with my imagination and wondering what to say and how to say it.

"See this neat little patch. Notice how carefully it's done?"

"Yes, sir," I said.

"See all these other shirts, hanging each on its own hanger, perfectly laundered?"

"Yes, sir," I answered, looking at still another row of other shirts, belonging to Theodore Collins's son, all of them also washed and ironed.

"This," Dad said, "is only one of the thousands of reasons why I think your mother is a very wonderful person. And just look at this! There are over a score of stitches in this one little patch. Your mother's hands made every one of them!"

He stopped talking for a minute, while I stood looking at what he was seeing and trying to think what he was thinking and was remembering that Mom's same hands had been used not just for stitching but also for switching. And what would she do and say when she found out about my unwashed and unironed shirt out in the toolshed?

I quoted to Dad an old quote, saying, "'A stitch in time saves nine.'"

Dad started swinging himself into the shirt again as he answered me. "Not *nine,* son. A stitch in time used to save nine, but it doesn't anymore. Not nowadays. It only saves *five* in this day and age." He grinned to let me know he thought he had thought up a pretty bright remark. Then he added in a sober voice, "Your mother, Bill, is a great woman. Truly great!"

His voice was so serious—in fact, it almost had tears in it, it was so husky—that I found myself swallowing a lump in my throat. He went on to say something else, which was, "You heard what she said back there in the living room when she saw the rainbow. That's one reason why she's great. Your mother worships God. And that would make any woman great."

I started to say, "Yes sir," but the words stuck in my throat.

Just that second there was a sound of somebody's dress swishing through the door into the room, and Dad's kind-of-shining eyes left the row of shirts and looked at Mom herself, who had just breezed in.

"What," she asked, "are you two youngsters mumbling about?"

"Secrets," Dad said and started to button the shirt from the top.

He got stopped by Mom, saying, "Let me see your neck a minute. You've been working in the hay, you know."

A small frown crinkled Dad's forehead just above his nose and his shaggy brows. Then he said, with a grin under his reddish-brown mustache, "I just scrubbed it less than four minutes ago. I'm not even dry behind the ears yet."

"That," Mom answered him, "is what I've always thought!"

Dad let her examine his neck to see if it had hayseed on it, then all of a sudden he whirled around, and before Mom could have said "Jack Robinson Crusoe," he was giving her a half-savage hug—trying to, anyway. Mom was like a slippery fish that didn't want to stay caught, and Dad was like a fisherman who wouldn't give up.

What was going on didn't seem any of my business so I went on out to the kitchen and saw a lonely looking towel hanging beside the dish drainer filled with discouraged dishes, just washed but not dry yet. I started drying them.

I had all the plates dried before Mom came swishing into the kitchen, and I heard her grumbling something to herself about having to put her face back on again. Then her tone of voice changed, and she exclaimed to me, "Your *hands!* You're sure you washed them before—"

She needn't have worried. I knew from having been told maybe a thousand times in my life that a boy's hands had to be washed before he ate, after he ate, and again before he dried dishes. My hands were all right.

But for some reason, my neck wasn't—not the back of it or the place behind my ears, which a boy never sees and his mother does. It wasn't any ordinary farm dirt Mom discovered, so when I started to explain what it was and how come, I found myself in the middle of the story of the shirt in the newspaper in the toolshed.

"I got my shirt dirty putting out the fire," I started.

"*What* fire?" Dad came in with his shirt half buttoned to ask, and the look of his face and also of Mom's made me feel the way a mouse in a corner probably feels when a woman with a broom is after it.

"I can explain it better by telling you a story," I said, and before they could stop me, I was off, talking kind of fast. "It might even be our minister's fault," I said, "because ever since that sermon on how to rule your spirit, I've been trying to be kind to Shorty Long and not fight with him anymore, and—"

Before I had the story finished, we were all outdoors by the iron pitcher pump, and the new, wrinkled, smudged plaid shirt was lying unwrapped on the newspaper on the pump platform. Mom's elbows were on her hips, and the tail of Dad's clean, freshly ironed shirt with the neat little patch on its collar wasn't even tucked in.

I got my spirit under control as I explained —so calmly that it didn't seem like me. "This red-haired boy who was trying to control his spirit thought he could heap coals of fire on his enemy's head by putting out the fire that was about to burn up the enemy's tent. When he couldn't find anything to use to beat out the flames—and there wasn't any time to lose—he sacrificed his nice, clean, new plaid shirt."

I wound up by saying, "So the red-haired, freckle-faced boy was so happy he had ruled his spirit by not letting the fire burn up the tent, that he jumped on his bicycle and pedaled home as fast as he could. He wanted his parents to be happy, too, which he knew they would be if they ruled their own spirits when they found out about the . . . about—" I stopped for a second and pointed down to the wet mess on the pump platform, then finished "—about that down there!"

My story was over. I looked at Mom and Dad's faces, and there wasn't any thunder or lightning on either one of them.

I don't know why I thought what I thought right then, but I thought it anyway, and it was *"I set My bow in the cloud."*

The only thing was that honest-to-goodness rainbows nearly always came *after* there had been a storm. But the way my folks looked at me and then at each other, there not only wasn't any storm, but there wasn't even going to be any.

All Dad said was, "We'll send it to the cleaners. If they can't get the smudge out, you can wear it for everyday."

Just then we heard a noise out by the small wooden gate that leads into old Red Addie's hog lot, then a baby's all-of-a-sudden howling cry. It was Charlotte Ann, my cute little baby sister, whom, for a few minutes, we had forgotten. I saw her lying upside down with her chubby little legs waving in the air and her chubby arms doing the same thing. Her very pretty, freshly laundered pink dress, which she was going to wear to town, was still on her, but it was also in the rain-made mud puddle by the gate.

Just one second before both Mom and Dad started on a dash across the barnyard, I heard Dad grumble under his breath the Bible verse that begins, "He who rules his spirit . . ."

I stooped, picked up the unwrapped, unwashed, unironed plaid shirt and carried it back to the toolshed. I'd have to hurry to get my neck and ears washed and dried and my clothes changed so that, when Charlotte Ann and the rest of the family were ready, we could start to town. Before I could get to the toolshed door, though, the phone rang in the house, and I had to run to answer it.

On the other end of the line Poetry's excited voice exclaimed, "Lightning struck the big sugar tree down by the north road and killed all our horses! *It killed Thunderball too!*"

Then Poetry broke into sobs and couldn't talk.

His mother's voice cut in then and said, "That you, Bill?"

When I said yes—gulped yes, rather, because my mind's eye saw Poetry's beautiful pinto pony lying dead along with all their other horses under the big sugar tree—Poetry's mother said with tears in *her* voice, "Will you call your mother to the phone?"

It was a sad sight. All the Thompsons' horses, roan and sorrel and black and brown, were lying sprawled in different directions, half off and half on each other all around under the tree.

Poetry's folks and mine and Little Jim's father stood looking at the dead horses and at the long ugly gash on the tree's trunk where the lightning had struck and run all the way down to the ground.

Poetry and I were by ourselves about ten feet from the other horses, where Thunderball himself was lying. "I'll bet he didn't want to die," Poetry gulped and said. "See? He got this far away after he was struck, trying to *keep* from dying, and he couldn't."

"He knew we needed him," I said sadly.

How many times that spring Poetry had come galloping up the road on him and stopped in a cloud of dust at "Theodore Collins" on our mailbox. How many times he had let me ride Thunderball, too. It was a wonderful feeling, riding like a Western marshal after a horse thief or a cattle rustler, my shirt sleeves flapping in the wind, my mind imagining I was living in America's Old West, bringing law and order to the country.

Poetry's getting the paint pony had been one of the things that had started the gang playing different cowboy games. It had seemed for a while that the whole Sugar Creek territory was changed from an ordinary playground to a Wild West ranch.

But now Thunderball was dead, killed by lightning! Never again would I look down the road and see a streak of yellow and black and white, with a boy riding it, come flying like the wind toward our house. Never again would I feel as if I were riding a thundercloud across a windy sky.

After that terrible electrical storm I was a little more afraid of lightning than I had been, although Dad explained that there wasn't more than one chance in a million that any human being would ever be struck by it.

"It *does* strike tall trees more often than low ones," he also explained one day. "So if you boys ever get under a tree for shelter from the rain, be sure it's a low tree, not a tall one."

Hearing that, my mind took a worried leap down to Shorty Long's new tent, which I'd kept from getting burned by putting out a fire with my new plaid shirt. That tent was pitched not more than a few feet from the base of the giant cottonwood! What if there'd come up a terrible electrical storm sometime when Shorty and Tom were in the tent? What if lightning would strike the tall cottonwood, and after the storm we'd find two dead boys inside the tent!

Somebody ought to tell those ornery boys to move the tent farther from the tree.

As soon as I found out just *who* that somebody was—the actual person who was supposed to warn the boys about the danger they were in—I began having more trouble with myself again. One of Poetry's favorite poems, which he had given in a reading once at the Sugar Creek Literary Society, kept going round and round in my mind.

Part of the poem wouldn't leave my mind night or day and was the cause of my getting into a very dangerous problem that spring. It started out:

> The good little boy and the bad little boy
> Both live in the house with me,

But it is quite strange—I can look and look,
Yet only one boy I see.

The poem hadn't made much sense to me when Poetry had first quoted it, and it still didn't. Yet I knew that whoever wrote it must have understood what a boy feels like when he *wants* to do right and there is something inside him that tells him not to.

I kept remembering Dragonfly's Snatzerpazooka, whom Dragonfly pretended was an actual person *outside* himself. But my Snatzerpazooka was *inside* me. And he wasn't only just a part of me but *was* me—actually myself.

I wanted to tell Shorty Long to move his tent away from the tall cottonwood, but my stubborn little Bill Snatzerpazooka Collins wouldn't let me do it.

"You just plain shut up!" I yelled to me one afternoon. "I'm going to do it if I want to!"

The fight between me and me was going to have to stop, and I was going to stop it!

I never will forget a very important afternoon and night about a week after the storm that killed Thunderball and the other horses. I was still having trouble with Shorty and Tom on the outside and with myself on the inside. I knew the Bible verse "Everyone who hates his brother is a murderer," and I didn't want to be that, even if Shorty Long *had* stolen Tom from our gang and was making him into a meaner and meaner boy.

I was working for Dad "on the shares" that

spring. That meant I would hoe the whole potato patch all summer and dig the potatoes when they were ready, and then *half* the potatoes would be mine and the other half Mom and Dad's. I could do what I wanted to with the money I would get from my half when I sold them.

I finished hoeing the last row, then stopped, wiped my brow on my red bandana handkerchief, shoved the bandana into my hip pocket, swung the hoe over my shoulder and started for the creek. There was something very important I was going to do—important and also dangerous, only I didn't know about the danger at the time.

4

I wasn't exactly sure what I was going to do, but I did know *where* I was going to do it, if I did it.

It wouldn't take me long. I could be back in plenty of time to do the chores. I'd have to do them alone because Dad had gone to attend a farmers' convention in Memory City, where my aunt lived, and wouldn't come home till tomorrow. He and Dragonfly's father had driven there in our car.

It took me only a little over fifteen minutes to get to the big hollow sycamore tree near the mouth of the cave, which was also near where Dragonfly had buried his imaginary playmate. When I got there, I went inside the cave a few minutes, then came out and lazed around a little, thinking and arguing with the ornery little rascal who was the other me, who didn't care whether lightning struck a cottonwood tree or not. The place was pretty lonesome, almost like an actual cemetery, I thought.

Snatzerpazooka's grave was completely covered with dead leaves, and there was, I noticed, a bed of sweet williams growing where the wooden marker had been.

I could feel my set face, my pursed lips, and

tight jaw muscles as I walked around, thinking and wishing I were a better boy than I was.

Then all of a sudden I finished making up my mind to do something I'd come down there to do.

In a minute I had the leaves raked away and, in only a few minutes more, had a hole dug. It was not a big one, only about large enough to bury a cat.

"And now," I said to me—not the actual me, but the ornery me—"inside you go!"

I went through the motions of picking myself up and dropping me inside the hole, saying, "Ashes to ashes, dust to dust" and also "leaves to leaves."

Then, after the hole was filled, I raked the leaves back to make the place look the way it had before.

I stood for a minute, looking down and all around. Suddenly it was as though I had heard a voice from somewhere, a very different kind of voice and very kind.

I stood stock-still in my thoughts and listened in every direction, wondering and scared a little. I don't know why I thought what I did just then, but having lived around Sugar Creek with red-winged blackbirds and squirrels and all the pretty wildflowers and everything in nature, it was easy for me to think about the One who had made everything, how wonderful He was, and how He liked boys and all people enough to give His Son to die for their sins.

It seemed the heavenly Father was right

there and that He was trying to get me to listen to something extraimportant He wanted me to hear.

After a minute or two had passed and there wasn't any sound except the piping of the small frogs in the swamp and other nature noises, I decided it had been only my imagination. I hadn't heard any actual voice. Yet I knew that God Himself *was* there. He was everywhere anyway, our minister always said, but sometimes He seemed to be in one special place in a very special way.

My imagination picked me up and whisked me away, over the tops of the trees, high over the woods and the Collins family's house and farm, up the gravel road two miles to a middle-sized white church on the hill above Wolf Creek, across the road from the Sugar Plain School.

I was inside the church on a Sunday morning, sitting by the window and hearing again the sermon you already know about. That is, I was hearing part of it. My thoughts that morning had been getting interrupted by two or three meadowlarks that every now and then would let out their whistling mixed-up song, saying, "Spring of the year!" They were outside the east window somewhere, maybe in the meadow on the other side of the graveyard.

Part of the sermon stuck in my mind. It was, "If you're having trouble with yourself, be sure not only to reckon yourself to be dead to sin but also *alive to God!*"

I didn't understand it at the time. But the last three words had sort of pounded themselves into my mind like a nail being driven into a board.

Now as I stood beside the grave in which two Snatzerpazookas had been buried, it seemed I was supposed to get my mind made up that the *ornery* me was dead and the *actual* me was alive to God.

For several minutes there was a very wonderful feeling inside, as though I were up in the air somewhere like a boy's kite on a strong string.

And that's when I heard actual human beings' voices—boys' voices. Shorty Long's and Tom Till's!

I looked around for a place to hide. The cave was too far away for me to get to it without being seen. To run toward the swamp wasn't a good idea either, because that was the direction the voices were coming from.

Then I caught a glimpse of two straw hats bobbing along the path that leads from the swamp.

In a minute they would be there. Shorty Long, the worst enemy I had, who, if he found out what I had been doing, would think I was crazy. And Tom Till, the only half-good boy old hook-nosed John Till had, who once had been my friend and almost a member of the Gang, who used to go to Sunday school with me but who now was worse than a slave to bully Shorty himself.

The very wonderful feeling I had had in my heart flew away like a swallow darting out of our haymow through an open window. In the place where the happiness had been was a scaredy-cat feeling that made me want to hide.

There wasn't any sense in being afraid, but for some reason I didn't want either one of those boys to know I was there. They wouldn't have understood what I was doing even if they had seen me. But I didn't want them to see me *now.*

The big hollow place in the old sycamore, I thought. *I'll climb up and squeeze myself in, and they'll go right on past!*

Quicker than anything, I circled the base of the tree and in a second was working my way through the opening, which was as wide as a narrow boy and about three times as high. I'd been in it many a time, and so had the rest of the gang, except Poetry, who was too round to squeeze through.

But getting in today wasn't easy. It had been a little chilly that afternoon, and I had on my leather jacket. I did some of the quietest grunting I'd ever done in my life as I twisted, squirmed, and shoved myself inside.

And just in time! One split second after I'd gotten the last of myself squeezed in, the boys were there. Would they go on past? I wondered—and hoped.

They wouldn't, I found out another split second later. I saw Shorty Long's gray-green eyes boring up into mine and heard him exclaim, "Well, well! If it isn't the little boy who goes around jabbing holes into other people's cows! Well, well, well!"

I gritted my teeth in anger. He hadn't even appreciated what Mom and I had done that other summer when his shorthorn cow had eaten too much ladino clover and had gotten the bloat. I had done what I knew I had to do to save her life. With Mom's help, I'd plunged a trocar into the paunch of his blue cow to let out the gas, and the cow had lived.

For a while after that, Shorty Long had seemed to like me a little. But he wasn't the kind of boy that could really like anybody but himself, Poetry had once told me.

I looked out and down at him through the narrow opening in the sycamore and answered his accusation. "I saved your cow's life! The veterinarian said so himself, and you heard him!"

Just saying "veterinarian" reminded me of horses as well as cows and of Poetry's folks' dead horses lying sprawled on and off each other around the base of the sugar tree that had been struck by lightning.

And *that* reminded me of Shorty Long's tent under the extratall cottonwood on the other side of the creek. "I saved your cow's life last year, and now I'm going to save yours," I decided to say. "You boys ought to pitch your tent farther away from the trunk of that old cottonwood so if the lightning ever strikes the tree, you won't be two dead horses. That tree's too tall. Lightning strikes tall trees!"

Shorty's sarcastic answer through the sycamore tree opening was "And where would you suggest that we poor dumb animals move it?"

I had a hard time answering through my gritted teeth. But then I remembered something else Dad had told me about lightning. I said, "If you *have* to have it under a tree, which you don't because it's better for a tent to be in the sunshine, then put it under the big old ponderosa."

"That, sonny," Shorty jibed, "is also a tall tree."

"It's tall," I answered, "but it's a *pine.* Pine trees have resin in 'em and—"

Shorty Long chopped my sentence in two, not letting me finish what I had wanted to say. I was going to quote Dad's exact words, which were: "The resin in pines interferes with their efficiency as conductors, and makes them more safe!"

But Shorty's cut-in words were: "And *sycamore* trees, my dear, have scared boys in 'em."

The smirk on his face when he said that showed that he thought he had thought up a very bright remark. He turned to Tom and ordered, "Come on, let's get back to camp and get our barbecue supper started."

I thought I saw Tom's jaw set, as if he was being bossed and didn't want to be. He looked straight into my eyes for a second, then turned as though he was as much a slave as "my man Friday" in the story of Robinson Crusoe.

Anyway, I thought, as they started up the path toward the mouth of the branch, they didn't beat up on me, as I had said *I'd* do to Tom if I ever caught him alone anywhere without his brother or Shorty along.

From where I was now, I could look out and see Dragonfly's Snatzerpazooka's old grave and the place where, with my hoe, I had dug a hole the size of a cat and buried that part of myself that really needed burying.

Right that minute, though, while my temper was boiling at Shorty Long, it seemed I ought to have kept *that* part of me alive, so if I ever had to give Shorty a licking, I could do it.

As soon as I couldn't hear their voices any longer, I decided they were quite a ways up the creek, and I started to worm myself out of my hiding place. I was going to make a beeline for Poetry's house, tell him about the word-fight I had just had, then hurry on home to get the chores done. I'd have to do them all by myself tonight because Dad was away, I remembered. Maybe I could get Poetry to come home with me and help.

I worked my left wrist out to where I could see my watch, and it was almost suppertime that very second.

"Well, here goes myself out," I said to myself and started to squeeze sideways through the narrow opening.

I *started* to squeeze my way through the narrow opening. I managed to get my right arm and shoulder out, and my head out far enough so that I could see the ground below me, and there I stuck.

I mean *stuck!*

I couldn't get any farther out. My heavy leather jacket had made me too fat.

"All right," I said to myself. "If I can get this far *out,* I can get back in again. I'll take my coat off, and it'll be as easy as pie to get all the way out."

It didn't make sense that I could have worked my way *in* and now, seven minutes later, couldn't wriggle *out.*

I grunted and twisted and squeezed again and again. I still couldn't get any farther out, but I *was* getting back in.

A minute later I was all the way in. If I was going to escape from my narrow prison, I'd have to use more than muscles. I'd have to use my mind a little. I'd have to be calm, in spite of the scared feeling that was beginning to make me tremble.

What if I couldn't get out? There wouldn't be any supper, and I'd have to stand up all night.

Now to get my heavy leather jacket off. Down with the zipper, which wasn't easy, because I had to keep my elbows clamped to my side to do it.

And then's when I felt myself sweating and really scared. My prison was too narrow for me to work myself out of my coat. I wasn't going to be able to get it off!

It's a terrible feeling to be in a tight place,

not able to get out, to be all alone without anybody there to talk to, to know suppertime has come and gone, and your parents don't know where you are, or any of your friends. And nobody comes to rescue you, and your voice gets hoarse from yelling, and you're tired standing in such a cramped place and are sleepy. And you know your mother is worrying, and that worries you even more.

I couldn't even bend my knees enough to slump down a little to rest my tired leg muscles.

After a while the night noises from the swamp—the nicest noises a boy ever hears when there isn't anything to worry about—began to get on my nerves.

Fireflies were flashing their green lights on and off in the willows, the pickerel frogs sounded like a hundred boys snoring and the bullfrogs like calves learning to bawl, making the whole place seem like a ghosts' cemetery.

Every now and then a screech owl would let out a long, trembling *"Sha–a–a–a–ay!"* It was enough to scare the living daylights out of a boy.

Just then a night heron let out a squawking *"Quoke . . . quoke!"* as if he had been trying to swallow a frog and it had stuck in his throat. The heron was one of my favorite night birds. In the daytime the black-crowned night heron acts dopey, and if you happen to stumble onto his roost, he hardly knows you are there. He is a greenish black, his tail and wings and neck are the color of a field mouse, and his stomach and throat are whiter than the ivory keys on Mom's organ in our living room.

I stared into the moonlight in the direction of the dark swamp, and then all of a sudden there were what sounded like a dozen night herons all quoking at once.

I'll bet there are a hundred of them, I thought; and for a few seconds I wasn't worried but was myself again, enjoying nature as I always do when I'm where nature has a chance to prove how wonderful it is.

Then, for a few moments it was quiet, deathly quiet. What, I wondered, had stopped the frogs from piping and bellowing and the herons from quoking? What kind of fierce, savage-toothed, long-clawed, hungry wild animal might be stealing along through the swamp in the direction of a hollow sycamore tree with a boy in it?

There were different things I could have worried about, such as: Was anybody out hunting for me? Had anybody told anybody on our party line phone that I was missing? One thing was pretty clear in my dumb mind right then, and that was that whenever a boy is going anywhere away from home, he ought to tell one of his parents or a neighbor or *somebody* where he is going.

I worked my hands into my different pockets to see if I had anything in the collection of stuff I usually carry to give me an idea how I could get out of my narrow prison. But there wasn't a thing that could help.

I could feel everything there was: a buckeye, which I always carried with me; a little ball of string, maybe ten feet of it; a couple of fishing sinkers; several nails; eight Lincoln pennies I'd been collecting; two nickels and a dime; a stub of a pencil . . .

If I had a piece of paper, I could write a note, I started to think, then stopped. Who could carry a note to anybody?

I also had a key to our toolshed, and in my jacket pocket were two matches. My mind tried to figure out some way to use the matches to get a message to somebody. I knew that just inside the mouth of the cave were two or three candles on little rock ledges along the walls. If I had a candle, I could light it and could wave it back and forth outside the opening and yell, and maybe somebody would see it and wonder what on earth and come and help me out. But, of course, if I could get to the cave to get the candles, I would already be out!

Another crazy idea struck me. It was to light a match, toss it out into the dry leaves on the two Snatzerpazookas' grave, and there might be quite a brushfire. Neighbors might see it, Poetry's folks especially, come down to put out the fire, and would find me.

But a brushfire could also spread to some of the evergreens and burn up a lot of good timber. Also, and maybe even more important, because there were leaves all around the tree I was in, I might get smothered with smoke. I couldn't even use the knife I had in my right pants pocket—or could I?

An idea shot a thrill through me. I could *whittle* my way out. I could whittle and whittle and whittle away on one side or both sides of the entrance until it was large enough for me to squeeze through.

Poor Mom! I kept thinking. *She must be nearly wild with worry.*

I was almost frantic with worrying about Mom's worrying. She might even telephone Dad long distance and get *him* worried and make him come driving like mad through the night to join the search for me.

All the time, while I'd been thinking and trying to plan how to get out, I'd been sort of listening for the special Voice I thought I'd heard before I'd squeezed myself into the tree. I kept thinking about the boy Samuel in the Bible, who had heard an actual voice from God calling him by name. That was one of my favorite Old Testament stories.

And the Voice didn't come. Instead, all the time I'd been there, I'd just had to look out onto the moonlit covering of leaves on the small cat-sized grave I'd dug. But when I got the exciting idea of whittling myself out, I knew I had thought of a way of saving myself. God had used my own mind to give me the idea.

Hardly knowing I was going to do it—in fact, I *didn't* know it until afterward—I said, "Thank You for putting the thought in my mind. Now help me to make it work!"

I managed to get my knife out and the blade open. In the moonlit dark I started to work, slicing off small, thin slices of the entrance where it was too narrow.

Grunt and whittle and worry and whittle and . . . and then the knife slipped in my hand and out of my hand. And fell.

Had it fallen outside or inside? I wondered.

I worked my head out and looked down, but in the darkness I couldn't see the ground well enough to tell whether the knife was there. Even if it *was* there, I couldn't get it, I thought sadly.

Maybe it had fallen *inside.* If it had, I would just stoop down and—but I couldn't *stoop.* I couldn't bend my knees, and I couldn't reach down far enough to pick up anything off the floor of my narrow prison!

If I could get my shoe and sock off, I could maybe pick up the knife with my bare toes and bend my knee far enough to get the knife up to where I could reach down and get hold of it.

But how do you get your shoe untied and off when you can't reach it? How do—

My mind's questions were interrupted then by the sound of a twig snapping somewhere behind the tree. There was also the fast *crunch-crunch-crunch* of leaves being walked on by somebody or *something!* My heart leaped into my mouth.

Something! A tornado of shivers whammed into me and sent my head spinning. That was why the pickerel frogs had stopped their snoring and the bullfrogs their bellowing and the night herons their quoking! There was a wild animal of some kind snooping around!

I could see its shadow now, long, with four legs and a long tail, and it was snuffling at the ground all around where I had been walking.

I cringed and pressed myself back into my shelter as far as I could and stared into the darkness at the animal that was circling and snuffling at my trail. In another minute, it would be at the tree where I was—a hollow tree with an opening that was too small for me to get out of but plenty large for a wild animal's head to get in!

I gritted my teeth and stood cramped, trembling, and terrified.

Now whatever it was began to move quickly in a circle toward the shadows of the cave, where I'd gone before coming back to Snatzerpazooka's grave.

I was so scared and mixed up in my mind that I hardly knew what was going on. I was even more mixed up a second later when a flash of light came from somewhere like a star falling or a meteor streaking across the sky. It shone all around in a wide circle, then it focused on the dark mouth of the cave, lighting up the gray rock wall at the back of the entrance room. And lighting up something else.

I saw for a fleeting second two fiery eyes like coals from a stove, and the hairy face of a large animal of some kind. Then all was dark—the darkest dark you ever saw or felt.

5

Now what do you do at a time like that? What *can* you do?

Those burning eyes might be the savage eyes of a wildcat—even if there weren't supposed to be any in this part of the country. There had been a *bear,* once when there weren't supposed to be any—a fierce, mad old mother bear, which we'd killed ourselves. But you maybe know all about that if you've read the story called *Killer Bear.*

I kept on standing and cringing and staring and wondering. Almost right away there was the *crunch, crunch, crunch, crunch* of dry leaves again, as something or other came bounding out of the cave into the shadowy moonlight and began circling with its nose to the ground again all around where I had been moseying in the afternoon.

Now it was where I'd dug the cat-sized grave. I could hear it sniffling the way Circus's dad's hounds do when they're on the trail of a coon or some other animal.

At the place where the two Snatzerpazookas were buried, the animal began to whine and act in a hurry and dig as if it was very excited. Dig . . . dig . . . dig . . . dig . . . making the dirt fly. Some of the particles struck against the tree I was in, and one actually hit me in the face.

That's when a bright beam from a flashlight landed on the grave, and in its yellowish circle I saw a reddish-brown dog. The dog quickly turned to look back, and I saw a long drooping head and floppy ears. It was old Redskin, Dragonfly's bloodhound.

A split second later Dragonfly's own excited voice shouted, "Get away from there! That's Snatzerpazooka's grave. Stop that digging!"

Redskin stopped digging, sniffed the air, and quicker than anything was where I was, standing on his hind feet, his front paws on the trunk of the sycamore, whimpering. Then, as "still" trailers do when they've finally treed their quarry, he let out a long-toned, wailing bawl, followed by a half-dozen sharp, quick chops, as much as to say, "I've treed him! Here he is! Come and get him!"

And that's when I let out a yell that scared the daylights out of Dragonfly.

In only a little while I was out. It hadn't taken Dragonfly more than half a minute to find my knife. Also, he was carrying with him his Scout hatchet, as he did nearly every time he was out in the woods with the Gang, especially when we were hunting at night with Circus.

Dragonfly was a little disappointed because Redskin, who now was a grown-up dog with an even sadder, droopier face than ever, had trailed a boy instead of a wild animal.

But Redskin was happier than Charlotte

Ann on Christmas morning. He leaped and played around me, trying to make his master realize what an important thing he had done.

Dragonfly used a surly voice on his dog playmate, saying, "Can't you *ever* learn to trail a coon or a possum or a fox? I can't make any money catching *boys!* They're not worth anything!" Imagine that. *Imagine* it!

"I thought all the time he was on a hot coon trail," Dragonfly complained.

As soon as he knew I had to get home quick to stop my mother from worrying, we were both on our way, following in the path made by his bobbing flashlight. "Where'd he pick up *my* trail?" I asked.

"Down by the sugar tree where Thunderball was killed," he said. "He'd been following along behind me. Wouldn't even try to smell *anything* till we got *there.*"

I remembered then. That was where I'd left our orchard, had climbed the fence, and stood for a while looking down with my mind's eye at seven dead horses—and one beautiful black and white and yellow pony. There also, I had thought about the tall cottonwood towering above Shorty Long's tent.

Crunch . . . crunch . . . crunchety-crunch-crunch-crunch. Our four human feet and four bloodhound feet scrunched along through the night toward the mouth of the branch on our way to stop two mothers from worrying.

It'd have been worse if our two *fathers* had been home, I thought, and said so.

Dragonfly sighed and answered, "I sure hope they bring back from the farmers' convention a few ideas about how to keep crows out of a cornfield. I'll bet there were a dozen big black ones down in our bottom field gobbling the new corn sprouts this afternoon. I tried to get old Redskin to help chase them away, but he wouldn't. He's as dumb as Snatzerpazooka used to be."

That got us to talking about scarecrows being a good way to keep crows away, and before we reached our different homes, we had decided to call a gang meeting the very next day to *make* a scarecrow to string up along the creek at the edge of Dragonfly's father's cornfield. One of the branches of the river birch not far from the swimming hole would be the best place.

It was fun making the most ridiculous-looking scarecrow our six minds could design. We made the head out of a small flour sack, first stuffing the sack with sawdust, then using crayons to draw his eyes, a nose, and a mouth.

"He's got to have long hair!" Dragonfly emphasized. His voice was very bossy for a little guy.

"Why?" Circus asked. "We don't have any hair for him."

"Because," Dragonfly whined, "because he's a horse thief, and he has to wear long hair to cover up the place where the top of his ear has been cut off."

It sounded ridiculous, and most of us said so.

"I read it in a book," Dragonfly explained. "In the Old West, whenever a man stole a horse and the cowboys decided not to hang him for it, like they did most horse thieves, they'd just cut off the top of one of his ears and turn him loose."

Poetry, who had also read a lot about the Old West, broke in then and added, "He's right. Anybody with the top of his ear cut off for being a horse thief wouldn't want anybody to know it, so he would let his hair grow long enough to cover the cutoff tip."

From what Dragonfly and Poetry had just said, our plan sort of grew by itself, and before the scarecrow was half finished, we had decided to play what Dragonfly and Poetry had also read about in different books, a game called a "Cowboys' Necktie Party."

The way it was done in real Old West life was that whenever a horse thief was going to be lynched, they'd lead him on his horse up under the overhanging branch of a tree, tie one end of the rope around the thief's neck, and the other end around the overhanging branch. Then they'd drive his horse out from under him and leave him dangling by his neck. The cowboys who had just hanged him would race away on their own horses, discharging their guns back in the direction of the just-hanged horse thief.

Little Jim thought of something that for a minute almost spoiled our fun. He said, "Didn't they have a trial first, like they do in *America,* and prove he was guilty before they hanged him?"

I looked at the innocent face of the littlest member of the gang, who was the best Christian of us all. I noticed his fists were doubled up as if he was ready for a fight, as if he'd be on the side of the horse thief and would defend him if he could. I remembered then that his father was the township trustee and that he had an uncle in the city who was a judge.

Poetry let out a snort at Little Jim's question, saying, "The Old West *was* America. Part of it, anyway!"

Big Jim knew a little history, himself, and quite a little about the Old West, so he answered both Poetry and Little Jim. "It was an unwritten law in the Old West that a horse thief had to hang. But sometimes the mob spirit got into a group of cowboys, and they didn't bother to have a trial first. It wasn't right, but they did it anyway."

Big Jim called a meeting, then, and said, "We'll try this old scarecrow right now. Little Jim, you be the judge."

It wasn't much of a trial and didn't last long. Poetry was the defense lawyer. He argued that the poor old scarecrow hadn't done anything wrong to deserve to be hanged. He made quite a speech in his squawky, ducklike voice. We'd all seen a mock trial the year before at a meeting of the Sugar Creek Literary Society, which meets once a month in the school across from the church.

I felt proud of Poetry. He stood under the spreading branches of the Jonathan apple tree in our orchard, where we were having our trial, and with a dignified face—for a while, anyway—said to Little Jim, "Your Honor, it's the *crows* that are guilty of stealing corn, not this poor old innocent scarecrow, who never did a wrong thing in his life."

Dragonfly was what in trials is called a prosecuting attorney. "This is the *second* horse he has stolen," he said, scowling. "When he stole his first one, we just cut off his ear as a warning. But now he's got to hang! Look at his long hair! *You* know why he has long hair. He wants his cutoff ear covered up, that's why!"

And that is when we found out what was going on way back in the little guy's mind behind his mussed-up face. He said, "Snatzerpazooka's *got* to hang!"

The trial was interrupted then by the judge and the jury and all of us crying out, "Snatzerpazooka? He's already dead and buried, and we've burned his grave marker!"

With that exclamation from everybody in our imaginary courtroom, Dragonfly seemed to forget he was a lawyer. He gave us all a surly scowl, quick stooped, picked up a stone from the ground and hurled it toward the road. My eye followed it as it sailed all the way across and into the woods, landing with a *ker-plop* against the black bark of the wild cherry tree that overhangs the road itself.

"That," Dragonfly scoffed, "was when I was *little!* I just pretended he was dead. I just pretended I buried him down by the sycamore tree. But this time, we'll really hang him. Snatzerpazooka's got to *really* die!"

And that was that. The trial broke up, and we went on with the necktie party.

Mom let us have an old mop she didn't want anymore, so our horse thief could have long hair to cover his cutoff ear. It had been one of her favorite mops when it was new. It had also been one of my favorites. Many a time I had used it to scrub the kitchen floor when I should have been down along the creek with the gang. But a boy can't let his mother get by with doing all the housework herself all the time, when that same boy's muscles need strengthening by pushing a mop.

The scarecrow was finally finished, and we faced the problem of how to carry him. It was quite a way from our orchard all the way down through the woods and along the bayou and the creek to the swimming hole and the river birch by Dragonfly's dad's cornfield.

"Put him on his horse," Dragonfly said. "Make him ride the horse he stole. Here, Bill. You look the most like a horse."

I scowled and frowned down at the end of my freckled nose. It didn't look any more like a horse's nose than anything.

To show the gang I could take a kind of

ornery joke without getting angry, though, I picked up our stuffed dummy, set his stuffed-with-straw overall legs astride my shoulders and took off on a gallop toward the orchard gate, getting there first. I stopped to rest in the shade of the big cherry tree, whose blossoms had a million petals on them, some of which had already fallen and were like snow on the ground.

In a month or so there would be ripe cherries on the tree, and it would be the robins that would need a scarecrow—except that robins don't scare easily.

I was puffing pretty hard, I noticed, so I complained about not wanting to be a stolen horse carrying a horse thief.

We decided two could carry Snatzerpazooka better than one, so Big Jim and Circus made a four-hand seat, and pretty soon we were on the way to the iron pitcher pump where we would give our thief a last drink of water before his execution.

At the southwest corner of the house, Poetry, in a mischievous mood, rushed over to our rain barrel and, looking in at the brownish water, started to yell one of my favorite poems:

"You can't holler down my rain barrel!
You can't climb my apple tree!
I don't want to play in your yard,
If you won't be good to me!"

Then he let out a war whoop down into the half-empty barrel. It sounded so much like a ghost's voice that it sent a shower of shivers all over me.

Inside our house, Mom, hearing the unearthly, bloodcurdling scream, came rushing to the back screen door just in time to see Big Jim and Circus carrying our dummy on their four-hand seat between them. I could see by her worried face that she was not only wondering *What on earth?* but also *Who?*

It took only a few words to explain what was going on and to get the worry off Mom's face.

I'd better tell you that the gang was always especially polite to Mom. Even I behaved better than usual when they were at our house. The reason wasn't only because Mom nearly always had a piece of pie for us, either. It just seemed natural for a boy to behave himself when there was a lady around.

She surprised us with a question. "Are you sure he is guilty?"

"We had a trial." Little Jim grinned up at her and added, "And I sentenced him to hang!"

Mom came all the way outdoors in her blue-and-white-flowered apron, walked with hands on her hips down the board walk to where we all were at the well platform. She looked down at our horse thief, with his crayon-made nose and eyes and mouth and ears, at the mop wig, which we'd sewed on with a darning needle. She surprised us again by saying, "Buffalo Bill Cody wore long hair; and Wild Bill Hickok, the famous marshal, had shoulder-length hair. But generally speaking, for a cowboy to wear long hair was frowned upon. In the Old West, if any man called another a Long Hair, he was sometimes answered with a quick draw and the roar of a six-gun."

Little Jim looked up at Mom, astonished, and blurted out, "How'd you know that? Who told you?"

I was thinking the same astonishing thing.

Mom's answer sounded sort of mysterious as she said, "Oh, I just overheard it on the phone this morning."

I knew what she meant when she said she'd "overheard" it. That meant that she had gone to the phone, maybe to call up somebody. She had lifted the receiver to listen to see if the line was busy, and it was, but she hadn't hung up right away.

"Who was talking to who?" I asked.

And Mom quickly answered, "Who was talking to *whom*, you mean."

"Yeah," Poetry said in his mischievous voice, "Bill wants to know who was who and whom was whom."

The twinkle in Mom's eye showed that pretty soon, if we took a little more time to get Snatzerpazooka his last drink, she'd go to the kitchen where the pies were and come back with a piece for each of us, which she did.

While Snatzerpazooka was resting against the post at the southeast corner of the grape arbor, his mop-covered flour-sack head twisted to one side, and while we were making short work of our six pieces of pie, Mom just stood on the board walk and smiled her favorite company smile. Then she said, "I suppose you're still interested in knowing who was who and whom was whom?"

Dragonfly sputtered an answer proudly. "I know who it was. It was my mother talking to Little Jim's mother. What did she say? Did Mother say I could go?"

That is when we really got the surprise of our lives. Mom answered little spindle-legged Dragonfly, saying, "Your mother said you could go."

"Go where?" different ones of us asked him, and he puffed up like a pigeon strutting around on the roof of our barn when he answered, "I'm going out West for the hay fever season. Out where the cowboys begin. I won't have to sneeze or have asthma for a whole month."

Little Jim came in cheerfully then with, "My father's taking Mother to the music festival at Aspen, Colorado, and Dragonfly's going with us."

I heard a sniffling noise beside me and, looking quick, saw Dragonfly's face starting to go into a tailspin. Then he took a deep, nervous breath, glanced toward the sun, shut his eyes, and let out a long blast on his sneeze horn, crying at the same time, "Snatzerpazooka!"

Then he looked all around and grinned, gave our scarecrow a kick with his bare foot, and said, "Come on, let's get him strung up!"

When we reached the front gate by the walnut tree, Mom called to us, "You boys get your party over as soon as you can. Don't forget the meeting tonight!"

I'd almost forgotten there was to be a meeting of the Sugar Creek Literary Society that very night. A famous chalk artist was going to draw colored pictures for everybody.

In a few minutes we had passed through our front gate, crossed the gravel road, and were on our way through the woods to the place where Dragonfly's imaginary playmate was really to come to an end.

Snatzerpazooka's mop wig covered not only his imaginary cutoff ear but his eyes as well. He looked as if he could scare the appetite out of any crow that got close enough to see him. Riding high on the four-hand seat between Big Jim and Circus, it seemed he *was* an actual honest-to-goodness horse thief.

It was a wonderful day, with the fragrance of wildflowers everywhere, warm sunshine spraying itself over the trees and bushes and the grass. It certainly felt fine to be alive.

All of a sudden I turned myself into a marshal of the Old West. With six-guns in their holsters at my belt and my rope on the pommel of my saddle, I galloped down the path on a beautiful all-white stallion.

I was hoping something very important, and that was that Little Jim's folks would not only take Dragonfly with them when they went to the Aspen Music Festival in Colorado, but that the rest of the gang would get to go too—me, especially.

Behind me, I could hear other fast-running steps. I took a glance over my shoulder, and it was Poetry, puffing hard, trying to keep up with my galloping horse. There was a sad expression on his face, though, and I guessed he was still heavyhearted on account of lightning having killed his wonderful pony, beautiful black and white and yellow Thunderball.

Behind Poetry was spindle-legged Dragonfly with Little Jim at his heels and, last of all, Snatzerpazooka on a handmade saddle between Circus and Big Jim.

We were six boys on our way to have a lot of brand-new fun playing a game we'd never before played. Also we were going to do a good deed by stringing up a scarecrow to save Dragonfly's cornfield from the crows.

Racing in and out between and behind and in front of us, was droopy-faced, flopping-eared, long-tongued Redskin, who maybe had saved my life only a day or so ago by trailing me to the hollow sycamore by the cave where the first Snatzerpazooka was supposed to have been buried and where I'd dug a hole to bury the ornery part of Bill Collins.

Panting and running and making a lot of boy noise, we reached the spring, crawled through the board fence, and went on the path to the swimming hole, where our boat was moored and near which was the river birch.

"As soon's we get our party over," Little Jim

exclaimed cheerfully, "we'll go in swimming and won't have to take any *bath* tonight."

The idea made me sad but also cheered me up a little. If there was anything I didn't like it was to take a bath before changing clothes to go anywhere.

In another minute the pretend necktie party would be on. The necktie party—and something else. I didn't know then that right in the middle of it we'd hear the shotgun shot you already know about, the one that scared us half to smithereens.

6

No sooner had we reached the swimming hole and the river birch, where we were going to string up our scarecrow, than we had to decide who was going to be the stolen horse.

The first thing I noticed was that there were four or five crows out in the cornfield having early supper. We quick plopped Snatzerpazooka down on the grass between the field and the swimming hole. Each of us grabbed up rocks and clods of dirt and yelled, "Scarecrow! Scarecrow! Scarecrow!" hurling our missiles out across the field at the black thieves.

I noticed, though, that Dragonfly was yelling a different word than the rest of us. He was screaming with a grin on his face, "Snatzerpazooka! Snatzerpazooka! Snatzerpazooka!"

The crows must have thought we meant business. They came to life as fast as crows can, then lifted themselves on their lazy black wings, and flapped their awkward way across the field toward the bayou and the woods beyond.

"You've got to be the stolen horse again!" Dragonfly said to me excitedly.

Quickly Big Jim had my lasso, which was a piece of Mom's new clothesline—there had been about ten feet too much when Dad strung it between the two posts standing between the house yard and the barnyard. Up the tree Circus went at Big Jim's orders. In no time one end of the rope was tied around the river birch branch, and about seven feet of the rest of the rope was dangling.

Big Jim himself was an expert at tying all kinds of knots. He made a bowline knot with a loop, which he put around Snatzerpazooka's stuffed flour-sack neck, while I, the stolen, freckle-faced horse, stood under the branch with Snatzerpazooka's stuffed legs across my shoulders.

"OK, men, get your guns ready!" Big Jim ordered. "The very minute his horse gets out from under him, everybody start running as fast as you can toward the spring, shooting back like they used to do in the Old West!"

In another tense minute, the stolen horse would shoot out from under the thief, which right that minute was astride my shoulders, and he would be left hanging and would never again be Dragonfly's imaginary playmate but would be a scarecrow instead.

We had to wait another half minute or two, though, because Dragonfly all of a sudden cried out, "Wait! Don't start yet!"

I stood there while he stepped back with his wooden gun in his hand and with a set face looked up at the thief. He said, "Good-bye forever! You used to be a good boy, but you turned out to be ornery, making me sneeze and sneeze and sneeze and *sneeze!* You're going to be a scarecrow from now on. I'm a magician, see?"

With that remark, Dragonfly walked toward me, keeping his eyes glued to Snatzerpazooka's head just above mine, holding his handmade wooden rifle like a magician holding a wand. He waved it a few times, then stepped back and stared and with a surly voice exclaimed, "OK, men! He's ready."

"OK, gang," Big Jim ordered. "Ready?"

"Ready!" most of us echoed.

"Don't start shooting," he ordered, "until Bill's out from under him!"

The second I—the horse—was free from my load, I quick changed myself from a stolen horse into a cowboy and was on my beautiful, white, imaginary stallion, galloping down the path toward the spring. All of us were yelling, *"Bang . . . bang . . . bang . . . bangety-bang-bang-bang!"*

And that is when we heard, right in the midst of our yelling, the explosion of an actual gun, which I told you about in the first chapter of this story. It was a very loud, startling explosion from somewhere or other behind us.

That is when we'd all stood and stared, and Dragonfly had looked back and stammered, "L–l–look! Snatzerpazooka's down! His rope's broke!"

We argued for a minute as to whether the rope had really broken or whether the noose had slipped off his neck.

Then, after what seemed quite a long while of wondering what on earth, we crept back toward the river birch. My heart was pounding with honest-to-goodness fear. There wasn't anything make-believe about the way I felt.

In only about three minutes after we'd started back, we reached the base of the tree. Snatzerpazooka was sprawled on the ground, his head leaning against the curled bark of the trunk, his crayon-made eyes looking pretty spooky.

Above him was the frayed end of the rope that had been hanging him. Big Jim's noose was still around the ridiculous neck, with about a foot of rope still on it.

Sawdust was scattered all over, and there were holes in Snatzerpazooka's face as if somebody had driven in a dozen nails and then had pulled them out again. On one side of his head, where the cutoff ear was, there was a large torn place.

Little Jim cried out then, saying, "Look! Here's his wig—way over here!"

He stooped, picked up the mop we'd sewed on with a darning needle, and held it up for us to see.

What, I thought, *on earth!*

It was as plain as Dragonfly's crooked nose what had happened. That is, *part* of what had happened was plain. The rest of the excitement didn't get explained till later.

Big Jim came up with the first idea when he frowned, in order to look like a detective is supposed to look, and said, "While we were here, tying the noose and getting ready to string up our scarecrow, somebody was hiding nearby, spying on us."

"As soon as Snatzerpazooka was up and hanging and we were running and yelling, 'Bang—bang—bangety bang!' shooting our toy guns, the spy shot him with a *real* gun—a *shotgun.* See here? Some of the pellets struck him in the face, and some struck the rope, cutting it in two."

Circus, who knew a lot about guns, broke in with, "Whoever shot him had to be pretty close to him or the pellets would have been too scattered for enough of them to have blown a hole in the side of his face and knocked his wig off and cut the rope."

I felt my temper starting to catch fire at anybody who would do such a thing to our horse-thief scarecrow.

We looked at each other's surprised and half-scared faces, wondering what to do, when all of a sudden, there was another shot. I saw a puff of smoke over across the cornfield near the bayou. A few seconds later, I heard a crow let out a scared squawk. I also saw at the edge of the field over there a black-winged bird flopping along on the ground kind of the way a chicken acts when its head has just been chopped off and it's out in the backyard dying.

Then I saw something else. A boy about my size, wearing blue jeans and a striped T-shirt, shot from behind a low shrub, scooted in a half crouch out into the field, chased the crippled crow until he caught it, and stuffed it into the gunnysack he was carrying. In a second, almost, he was back behind the shrubbery that bordered the bayou.

"It's Little Tom Till!" several of us exclaimed.

"He's shooting crows for bounty, I'll bet," Poetry offered. "It was in the paper this morning. They're paying ten cents for every crow that's killed this month."

Dragonfly let out a hot-tempered explosion, crying, "Ten cents! Why, that little thief! That's my crow! He shot it in our cornfield!" Before any of us could have stopped him, that little rascal of a spindle-legged boy was like a barefoot arrow, skimming out across the field toward the place where we'd last seen Tom and his gunnysack with the crow in it.

It made me cringe to watch Dragonfly Roy Gilbert racing as if he was mad enough to bite a ten-penny nail in two, straight toward the place where a few seconds ago I'd seen Tom Till.

I'd seen Dragonfly in quite a few fights, and he was a fierce fighter. Also, I'd not only seen Tom Till in the middle of several fistfights but had been in one *with* him. In fact, my nose had been on the other end of one of the hardest-knuckled fists a boy ever felt.

That fight was the nose-bashing Battle of Bumblebee Hill in the story *Killer Bear.* Tom was a fierce fighter, but Dragonfly was heavier, had a hotter temper, and he'd soon make short work of the little guy, I thought. I felt my forehead getting as wrinkled as old Redskin's, who, like greased red lightning, was loping in long leaps after his master.

"We'd better go stop the fight before it starts!" I cried excitedly to the rest. I leaped on my white horse to race after Redskin and his crooked-nosed owner. I felt almost as if I was running headfirst into some kind of battle myself, like a Western marshal on the way to save a friend from getting killed or maybe to stop two friends from hurting each other.

As I galloped across that neck of land to the bushes that bordered the bayou, I saw myself the hero of a real-life cowboy story, flying like mad on my white horse with the rest of the gang on their own horses following me. Dust was rising from our horses' galloping hooves, and we were making short work of the distance between us and the scene of whatever trouble we'd find when we got there.

My hair was long and beautiful, streaming down on my shoulders, because I was Wild Bill Hickok himself, the famous marshal and gunfighter. In its holster at my right side was my notched six-shooter, which had turned itself from a wooden gun made out of an old shingle into a colt revolver with six honest-to-goodness cartridges.

I got to the grassy border in only a few seconds. Poetry got there right behind me before any of the rest. We heard a savage voice I certainly didn't expect, and for a moment I didn't recognize whose it was. That same voice barked, "Stop where you are! Don't move. Get your hands up!"

"Shorty Long!" Poetry cried beside me.

And it was. Shorty Long, the only boy I ever saw who was as heavy as Poetry and who was as hard to get along with as any bully anybody ever saw or heard.

It was what else I saw that made me cringe. Standing not more than five feet from the edge of the bayou was little Tom Till, holding the gunnysack with the crippled crow in it. Tom held the bag shut with both hands. Beside him, both his small hands above his head and looking like a scared rabbit afraid to move, was Dragonfly.

Behind a fallen log, standing with one foot on it and with a double-barreled shotgun held as if he would use it if he had to or wanted to, was mean-faced, set-jawed, glinting-eyed Guenther Shorty Long, the boy I'd licked a few times in fights, and the life of whose blue cow I'd saved one summer.

A second later there were three more boys beside and behind me, all of us getting stopped stock-still by Shorty Long's fierce face and shotgun. The gun wasn't pointed at us but was held ready to point if Shorty would have been dumb enough to actually do such a dangerous thing.

All of a sudden from beside me there came one of the sauciest voices I ever heard, kind of high-pitched and trembling but crying, "You great big coward! Holding a gun on us! You *drop* that and fight like a man!"

It was Little Jim, the littlest one of us and, as I've already told you, the best Christian of us all.

I don't know what was in that little mouse-faced boy's mind, but when I saw the look in his eyes, I knew he was in his own little world of imagination. He had maybe seen or read a story somewhere in which the hero hadn't been afraid of the villain's gun in spite of its being pointed at him.

Before anyone could stop him, Little Jim Foote, with his eyes glinting back at Shorty Long, started on a slow, stiff-legged walk—his elbows out, his fists doubled up, his smooth little jaw set, his lips pursed—straight toward the big boy standing behind the fallen log.

"You're a *coward!*" Little Jim said again and gritted his teeth.

What he said and the way he said it did something to Dragonfly, the next-to-the-littlest one of us. While Shorty Long's eyes were focused on Little Jim walking toward him, Dragonfly lowered his arms, doubled up his own fists, and shouted, "You great big bully! You're afraid to drop your gun!"

I saw red anger flash into Shorty Long's eyes, saw his finger on the trigger of the shotgun twitch, and I knew it would be as easy as anything for him to get excited and that one of us might get killed.

There we all were with our toy guns—some plastic, some handmade out of wood, some of tin or other metal—and standing before us in a mad mood was a boy who didn't like us anyway, and he had a real gun!

My own temper was telling me to put my

muscles to work, to watch my chance, to make a flying leap toward the mean-faced boy, seize his double-barreled shotgun, thrust it aside, and land a few fierce, fast furious fists on his broad face. For a second, in my mind's eye I had already done it. I had made short work of Shorty Long. But it was only in my mind's eye. I had better sense than to risk my life in such a foolish move.

Big Jim took over then. He said, "We're not going to be fool enough to jump you! And we know you wouldn't be a bigger fool and pull that trigger! But we'd like to know something!"

All this time little Tom Till was holding the gunnysack with the crippled crow in it, struggling as a chicken in a gunnysack does, trying to get out.

Shorty Long's sarcastic voice answered Big Jim, saying, "Oh, so you admit you're all a bunch of ignoramuses and you don't know a thing."

That tightened Big Jim's muscles and his fists and put fire in his eye. I thought for a second he was going to fly into the kind of action I'd seen him fly into before when there was a boy who needed a licking. But he didn't. Instead, he spoke with hot but controlled words. "We want to know who shot down our scarecrow. Did you do it?"

A saucy smirk spread across Shorty Long's face as he answered, "I am like George Washington. I cannot tell a lie. I did it with my little double-barreled shotgun! You boys were hurting our business. Tom Till and I are partners in a new business venture. I shoot the crows; he is my retriever. He goes out and gets them for me, and I give him three cents out of every ten-cent bounty we get.

"We got six crows yesterday, and we aren't going to stand for any gang of boys putting up a scarecrow to scare our crows *away*."

Then Shorty Long's hands tensed on his gun, a hard look came into his eyes, and he barked, "You can all get yourselves out of here—and *fast*. Now *git!*" He waved the long, double-barreled gun threateningly.

I caught little Tom's eye then, and he was sending some kind of message to me, trying to say something. His lips moved, and he gave me several secret signs, which I couldn't read.

It looked as if, even if he was a partner of Shorty Long, he wasn't glad of it and was on our side.

Dragonfly's saucy little scared voice, with tears in it, said then, "If you shot the crows in my father's cornfield, they belong to me!"

And Little Jim piped up with a Bible verse out of the Ten Commandments, "You shall not steal!"

We weren't getting anywhere, but it was better shooting at each other with words than with bullets.

"I said," Shorty Long thundered, "I said, get yourselves out of here!" and he took a menacing step over the log in our direction.

Big Jim, who was in front of the rest of us, stood without moving a muscle.

Something happened then that sent us all into flying action, and in a split second things were *really* happening. I hadn't noticed what Circus was doing and didn't have any idea what else he was going to do until he had done it. But all of a sudden he wasn't there, and then I heard him let out a half-dozen raspy-voiced caws that sounded like a crow cawing.

Quick as a flash, Shorty Long swung his gun around, while his eyes circled the sky, his body turning at the same time.

And that is when Big Jim jumped him. Big Jim's muscles, made strong from working hard on the farm, wrested the gun from Shorty Long almost before you could have said, "Jack Robinson Crusoe." I expected any minute, though, while the scuffling was going on, to hear a deafening explosion as the gun went off.

Dragonfly, angry and excited, leaped into the scuffle as soon as he saw a chance to get in without getting hurt. He whammed Shorty Long's stomach a few times but got stopped by Big Jim's ordering him, "No fighting! Stop!"

Dragonfly stopped, and Big Jim whirled out of the way of Shorty's arms as they reached for the gun.

"Hold him, boys, while I unload this!" Big Jim ordered.

Afterward, I found out I was one of the first ones to get to Shorty. A sore place on my jaw was proof he had gotten to me also.

In the midst of our scuffle, Shorty Long went down, with quite a few of us on top of him, not more than seven feet from the edge of the bayou pond.

While we were holding him, Big Jim broke open the shotgun and drew out two shells, one from each barrel. Resting the gun on his left arm and holding the two shells in his right hand, Big Jim looked down at Shorty Long's flushed face and said something every boy in the world ought to hear.

"*Never* point a gun at anybody, loaded or not! Hundreds of people have been killed by guns that weren't supposed to be loaded. If those guns had been pointed *away* from people when they discharged, lives would have been spared."

What Big Jim was saying had already been made a rule of the Gang. The only guns we ever pointed at each other were toy guns that couldn't shoot. There wasn't a one of us that would even think of using a real gun in our games. We wouldn't be that dumb.

Shorty Long was gritting his teeth at what he was having to hear. Then he startled us by saying, "I've got three other shells in my pants pocket. Bill, here, is lying on them. How about letting me up?"

That, I tell you, scared me. What if while we were wrestling with our prisoner, something had caused those shells to explode! What *if*?

It was as dangerous as playing with dynamite! I certainly stopped lying where I'd been lying and scrambled quickly onto my knees. But I kept on using both hands with all my might, keeping Shorty's right arm pinned to the damp, dank-smelling ground. We were, in fact, lying in a patch of catnip, which, getting crushed like that, smelled like a boy's breath when he is chewing peppermint gum.

What to do now? was the question. It was a pretty bad situation. But in another moment it was worse. Right then we heard the voice of somebody calling, "Guenther! Where are you?"

It was the worried, angry, thundery voice of Shorty Long's father.

I hardly had time to remember the first time that same father had come looking for his boy in the story *The Blue Cow.* We'd been in a scuffle with his son, and Shorty had yelled for help and—but that's the *other* story.

The fatherly, thundery, worried, angry voice wasn't more than fifty yards from us somewhere up at the east end of the bayou.

Just then Shorty let out a scream that socked me in the face and ear and almost deafened me. "Help . . . help . . . they're killing me! H-e-l-p!"

There was a sound of heavy feet running through the underbrush. Then the bushes parted, and Shorty's two-hundred-pound, round-in-front father came into view. I noticed he was wearing the same sport shirt I'd seen him have on before—a bright gold color with bunches of purple grapes all over it. He was also wearing his small, sporty mustache, too small for his big face. *And* he was carrying a fierce-looking beech switch.

Seeing him, Shorty started yelling again, "Help! Help! They're killing me!"

7

Seeing his red-faced, struggling son wallowing in the catnip bed like a tied hog, with five boys holding him down, and Little Tom Till standing close by with his crippled crow, and Big Jim standing with a double-barreled shotgun only a few feet from us, Shorty Long's father stopped and demanded, "*What* is going on here?"

Several of us started to talk at the same time, saying things that couldn't have made sense to anybody who didn't know what we knew. Dragonfly's smallish, excited voice started our explosion of words as he began, "He shot down our scarecrow, and he's been shooting my father's crows and stealing them and selling them, and they're my crows!"

Big Jim's words, coming out at the same time, were "He held a loaded gun on us!"

Poetry's ducklike voice came out with, "He broke up our necktie party!"

Little Jim chimed in excitedly, "It's wrong to steal! The Bible says, *'You shall not steal.'*"

I must have sounded as if I was trying to defend myself for having done something wrong when I grunted out, "I was lying on his pocket, but I got off because it's dangerous to lie on three loaded shotgun shells!"

What on earth made me say that? I wondered, and so also must have Shorty Long's father. All our explanations must have seemed like five scarecrows talking at once.

"Stop! All of you! Let my boy up this minute! Guenther, get up!"

His voice was so sharp that *I* started to obey but got stopped by Big Jim ordering us, "Don't move! Keep him down! I want to explain a few things!"

And Big Jim *did* explain. In a fast, sharp-talking speech that made me proud of him, he said to Shorty Long's father, "Your boy's too young to be out carrying a shotgun and shooting it, and he ought to know better than to point it at human beings!"

Just then our prisoner came to teeth-gritting life. He started to struggle fiercely, crying for help again and demanding, "Let me up! You—you—"

"Not yet!" Big Jim ordered us. He stooped, shoved his hand into Shorty's right pants pocket, took out three shells, then exclaimed with a grunt, saying, "They've already been shot!" Big Jim held out to Shorty Long's astonished father the three empty shells and the two unshot ones. He handed him the gun also and said to us, "All right, boys, let him up."

It wasn't easy for me to obey. It would have been easier to have landed a few fierce fast fists first. But I didn't, for just before I took my weight off my prisoner's arm, which I'd been keeping pinned to the ground, I caught a glimpse of Guenther Long's father's face, thundery with anger. I saw also the beech switch and realized that Shorty might not need any more punishment than he was going to get.

Remembering that my own Snatzerpazooka was supposed to be dead and buried in a cat-sized grave by the sycamore tree, I made myself try to defend Shorty by saying to his father, "Maybe he didn't know any better. Maybe if he'd been taught at home how to behave himself and not to carry a gun and point it at people—"

That was as far as I got. I was interrupted by the very firm voice of the man in the golden shirt with the purple grapes on it, who roared, "You, young man! Leave our son's training to his parents! Now get going—all of you!"

And we got!

First, though, I decided to try to win little Tom back to ourselves by saying, "Come on, Tom! Bring your crow and come with us!"

But Shorty Long made a dive for Tom. He grabbed the gunnysack with the crow in it, yanked it away from him, and left a sad, freckle-faced little guy standing as though he didn't have a friend in the world.

Shorty and his father were growling something to each other as they stomped up the border of the bayou toward their home.

Tom sniffled a little. He looked first after Shorty, then at all of us in a kind of worried circle. And then, turning, he struck out across the cornfield toward where Snatzerpazooka was lying propped against the curled bark of the trunk of the river birch.

In a flurry of flying feet I was off after Tom Till. I had to try again to win him back into the gang and away from Shorty Long. I also wanted to invite him to go with us to the Literary Society to hear the chalk artist. Tom was especially good in art in school and might be glad to go.

Well, he was a fast runner and already had a head start.

"Wait, Tom!" I yelled to him. "I want to ask you something!"

But he didn't wait. When he reached the river birch, he didn't even bother to look down at Snatzerpazooka but swerved onto the path that led down to the spring.

"Wait!" I yelled again. "I want to tell you something *important!*"

I didn't bother to stop to look at the scarecrow, either, but cut across the dust of the cornfield rising from Tom's flying feet. Small particles of dirt hit me in the face as I followed.

In a few seconds I had reached the path that twisted through the weeds and tall sedge, my heart pounding with excitement and with my plan to take Tom with us that night, if his folks would let him. It seemed that now I ought to try extrahard to be his friend.

And that's when I ran into something in the path. However, it wasn't a *thing*. It was a human being as big as Big Jim. He sprang from behind the trunk of an oak tree, grabbed me around the waist and hurled me to the ground, where I struck my head on a root and for a second couldn't see anything but stars.

But I could *hear* everything: a crow cawing somewhere, a half-dozen robins scolding because we were on their territory, and a surly voice accusing me, "You let my little brother alone, do you understand!"

It was the angry voice of Big Bob Till, Tom's brother, the meanest boy in the whole neighborhood except for maybe Guenther Shorty Long, and the fiercest fighter except Big Jim.

He stood glaring down at me, kicked at me with the toe of his heavy shoe, then ordered, "Get up and get back with your own gang!"

Before I knew what I was doing, I'd reached out with both hands, grabbed Bob Till's ankle, and was holding onto it for dear life, yelling as Shorty Long had done, "Help . . . help . . . help!" to the gang to come to the rescue.

And the gang came. There was the pounding of ten galloping feet racing down the path toward me, and voices calling, answering my own frantic calls.

Even as I struggled, holding on like a bulldog to Bob Till's ankle and getting whammed in different places on my body by Bob's fists, I saw the bushes part up the path and Big Jim burst through on the run, with the rest of the gang tumbling after.

Bob saw them, too. With a mighty heave, he yanked his foot free, leaped over a pile of drift, and disappeared in the general direction of the creek. His flight made a very exciting sound as he crashed through the underbrush.

The stars I'd been seeing were gone, but there was a throbbing in my head where it had struck the protruding tree root.

I explained what had happened, and why, and for a few minutes we all stood looking at each other and talking everything over. Then Big Jim said, "Let's go back and start where we left off. Let's get the scarecrow up again."

I went kind of dazedly along with my throbbing head, thinking what a failure I had been and discouraged that I hadn't done a very good job of ruling my spirit. I was as mad as I'd ever been in my life and was ready to plunge headfirst into the first fight that came along.

A red-haired fiery-tempered boy with a spirit like mine would have to have help from somewhere if he was going to act like a Christian boy was supposed to.

There wasn't a one of the gang, not even Poetry, my closest pal, to whom I could explain how I felt inside and why.

For a minute I felt tears getting mixed up with what I was seeing, and I must have let out a kind of groan, because Little Jim, who was right behind me as we hurried toward Snatzerpazooka at the base of the river birch, asked, "Does your head hurt pretty bad?"

"My head?" I answered. "Not too bad!"

It wasn't my head. The pain was way down inside somewhere. In fact there was a great big ache in my chest just above my stomach. It wasn't like any kind of pain a boy gets when he's been hit in a fight or fallen down and bumped his knee or stubbed his toe. And it was all mixed with a sad feeling that weighed about a hundred pounds.

Bob Till's grabbing me and whamming me to the ground meant that *he was home again* from having been away a few months. Now we'd have more trouble, and it'd be harder than ever to get Tom to be one of us again.

Well, in a few moments we would come out into the open and would be at the lynching place. I didn't have any heart to go on with the necktie party. In fact, none of us probably felt like it. We would just string up our scarecrow and get on back home to get ready to go to the potluck dinner at the school and the Literary Society afterward. I was already hungry enough to eat a bear.

Just then, up ahead of the rest of us, Dragonfly let out a yell. "He's gone! Snatzerpazooka's gone!"

That sent the rest of us into a gallop toward the river birch—and not on imaginary horses, either.

Dragonfly was right. There wasn't any ridiculous-looking scarecrow with his missing wig and spattered face. There was only the tree, a mashed-down place in the grass where he had been, and sawdust scattered all around the base of the tree.

What on earth!

We looked all around under the bushes,

knowing Snatzerpazooka couldn't have moved himself.

Then we learned something else when Dragonfly, who was searching the area down by the swimming hole, cried out excitedly, "Hey, gang. Come here! Our *boat's* gone too. Somebody's stolen our boat!"

Snatzerpazooka was gone! The boat was gone. A scarecrow made out of old clothes stuffed with straw and sawdust, with a rope around his neck, half his face blown away with a shotgun blast, *couldn't* have gotten to his feet and walked or run or flown away! Nor could a rowboat, which had been chained to the maple tree at the edge of the water, have unchained itself and rowed itself down the creek.

"What," I said, "on earth!"

In a flurry of flying feet, the rest of us were where Dragonfly was, looking in every direction to see what we could see.

"Listen to that!" Big Jim cried.

I didn't have to listen in order to hear it. It was a long, low rumbling like a wagon or a car crossing the board floor of the Sugar Creek bridge about a quarter of a mile down the creek. Many a time in the middle of the night, I'd been wakened by that noise. It was as much a part of our life at Sugar Creek as other familiar sounds such as the *"Sha-a-a-ay"* of a screech owl or the crowing of a midnight rooster.

But Circus exclaimed, "*Thunder!* It's going to rain!"

We all looked around in different directions to see if we could see any big white cumulus clouds, looking like packs of wool, which is nearly always what you see in the late afternoon when a thunderstorm is coming up.

Dragonfly's mind was on his scarecrow, though, and on the missing boat. It was his dragonflylike eyes that spotted the boat first. "Look!" he cried, pointing downstream. "There it is, floating with its oars in it, away down in front of the spring!"

Circus was quickly halfway up a sapling near the shore, shading his eyes and looking. He cried, "There's somebody in it! There's a *man* in it, lying down!"

I could see our weathered old rowboat myself, away out in midstream. And lying in the bottom, with one arm hanging over the gunwale and dragging in the water, was the figure of a man.

"It's our scarecrow!" Little Jim cried. "He's come to life and is having a lazy afternoon boat ride."

I happened to be looking at Dragonfly that second, and a startled expression came over his face.

"That's it!" he cried excitedly. "It's Snatzerpazooka come to life again!"

Then he started to yell what he was saying. "In the Old West, if they lynched a man, and one of the bullets they shot back at him cut the rope, his life was saved. He never had to be hanged again!"

Dragonfly was so superstitious, partly

because his mother was that way, that it was sometimes hard to tell whether he was *really* believing something or just pretending.

"Ridiculous!" Poetry scoffed. "Whoever untied our boat threw old Snatzerpazooka into it, shoved the boat off, and let it go."

"Bob Till!" I grunted and for some reason felt my head-throbbing and my temper coming to life.

Right that second it thundered again, this time a louder, longer, closer rumble, and we knew it was going to rain for sure.

But we couldn't let our boat drift away. We'd have to get it and tie it up at the shore somewhere, or it'd float downstream to the island below the bridge. If, when it got to the island, it took the *left* channel around it, it would have a long half mile of marshy, swampy shoreline to follow, and we'd never be able to stop it. It might go on downstream for miles and with our shotgun-blasted scarecrow in it!

Just then a cloud of dust was whipped up from the cornfield behind us, blowing across where we were, and a strong wind ruffled the surface of the water of our swimming hole. The leaves and branches in the trees all around and overhead began to rustle and toss, and it looked like an old-fashioned Sugar Creek storm was almost here.

"We've got to get the boat tied up before the storm strikes!" Big Jim cried, and his cry was an order. He started on the run down the path toward the spring, with all of us trailing as fast as we could.

The wind was in our favor. It was at our backs as we ran. It was also in the boat's favor, for out in midstream, where there wasn't anything to break the wind, the waves were pushing it along fast. And I mean *fast.* Almost as fast as it could have drifted in a spring flood. It was the first race I had ever had with a runaway boat. It was also a race to beat a storm.

Back over his shoulder came another order from Big Jim. He called, "Don't anybody stop at the spring for a drink! If we can get to the bridge before the boat does, maybe we can rush out onto the neck of sand there and, if it passes close, reach out and pull it in!"

Plop . . . plop . . . squish . . . squish . . . our twelve bare feet flew down the path. Plunging along its winding trail, dodging branches or ducking under them so that none flew back and hit the face of anybody that was behind us, we flew like Santa's reindeer were supposed to have flown in the poem "The Night Before Christmas."

For a fleeting minute, my imagination changed me from a cowboy on a galloping white stallion into white-whiskered Santa Claus himself, sitting in a sleigh jammed with toys, sailing through the sky with sleigh bells ringing, "more rapid than eagles," as the poem goes.

A glad feeling welled up inside in spite of my still-aching head where I'd bumped it on the tree root, and I yelled toward the other racing gang members:

"Now Dasher, now Dancer,
Now Prancer, now Vixen!
On, Comet! On, Cupid!
On, Donner and Blitzen!

"To the top of the porch,
To the top of the wall,
Now dash away, dash away,
Dash away all!"

Besides being Santa Claus in the sleigh, I was also riding a red-nosed reindeer, and it felt fine to be alive. It really was a wonderful day, even if it was going to storm almost any minute.

Hurry, hurry, hurry, *hurry!*

Circus, our acrobat, being the fastest runner as well as best in nearly all sports, was ahead of Big Jim now.

Quick as anything, we were through or over the board fence by the spring, up the incline, past the leaning linden tree, and galloping down a path that bordered the top of the cliff above the creek.

It looked as if we might make it to the bridge and down the embankment to the neck of land underneath just in time to reach out and stop the boat as it went by.

Right then, a blinding flash of lightning blasted Santa Claus and his reindeer out of the sky and turned him into a scared boy who at the same time felt a drop of rain strike him in his face.

Away up ahead, Circus called back to us, "It's *raining!* We can make it to the bridge and get under it for shelter. Hurry!"

And we hurried. Past the pawpaw bushes on our left, on to the rail fence at the north road, over the fence, across the road and down the embankment, under and in the dry just as the rain broke loose and started coming down in sheets.

But would we be able to stop the boat? I wondered.

8

The rain was so blinding that the sky itself seemed almost black. We could hardly see anything.

"There he comes!" Dragonfly cried in a whining voice. "Look at him lying there in the boat in the rain! He's g–g–g–getting w–w–w–wet!"

"Who cares!" Poetry squawked back. "He'd have been *all* wet hanging back there in the tree!"

"But he'd have been *dead* and wouldn't have known it," Dragonfly whined. "He's *alive* now!"

What a nonsensical idea—that is, if Dragonfly really believed it and wasn't just playing make-believe.

"Stop being a make-believe!" Little Jim ordered Dragonfly. "That's just an old scarecrow!"

Through the sheets of rain I could see the boat being whipped along in the strong wind. It was coming fast down the creek, but it was going to miss by fifteen or twenty feet the little sandy beach we were on. In only a few minutes it would blow past. Then we wouldn't have a chance to get to it at all. It'd go drifting on down to the island.

Our acrobat came to life then. "I'll get

her!" he declared in an excited voice. "I'll go out onto the bridge and drop down into her and row her in!"

He whirled and, like Dasher or Prancer or Comet or Vixen, was to the top of the embankment, and I heard his bare feet on the boards of the bridge as he raced out to the middle.

It was a bright idea, I thought. Both oars were in the boat. Snatzerpazooka was lying sprawled across one of them.

From under the bridge, we could see Circus working his way down over the side directly above where soon the boat would be. He had timed it just right. In a second now, the boat would be under him. Then he'd let go and drop into it.

It was as good as watching an acrobat at the Harvest Home Festival at Sugar Creek—except that I'd never seen one of them performing in a blinding rain, with thunder and lightning roaring around in the sky.

"Drop! Let go now!" Big Jim's voiced barked.

And Circus dropped.

That is, he dropped partway. But *only* partway!

"His overalls suspenders are caught!" Little Jim cried.

The boat with the dead or alive scarecrow in it went blowing on downstream. And away up above the mad water was Circus, hanging by his overalls, their suspenders hooked on the projecting edge of a wooden beam.

But that was only for a few scared seconds.

Fast as a firefly's fleeting flash, Circus worked himself around, struggled to reach back and up to catch hold of the beam, and pulled his body up to where he could unhook himself. Quicker than quick, there was our acrobat flying through the air with the greatest of ease straight down in an awkward sprawl toward the creek.

He landed all right, but not in the boat, which by that time was quite a few yards downstream.

There was a splash, which we could hardly hear or see for the blinding rain, and Circus was not only in the water but under it! He was right up again, sputtering and spitting creek water, and swimming toward us.

It was one of the most exciting minutes of my life. I stood cringing and yelling, along with all the other yelling voices beside, behind, and in front of me.

You'd have thought Circus would have been as mad as a wet hen, but he wasn't. Instead, he came crawling out of the water onto the shore, grinning like a friendly monkey and saying, "I won't have to take a bath tonight, maybe."

But Dragonfly was beside himself. He let out a yell and started to race down the narrow path that follows the creek only a foot or so from its bank.

Big Jim was after him at once and dragged him back into the shelter of the bridge. And that was that.

The rain kept coming down by barrelfuls for some time. Our battered old boat with Snatzerpazooka in it kept on drifting downstream toward the island. There wasn't any sense in any of us getting ourselves all wet trying to run ahead of it, in the hope it might drift near the shore so that we could stop it before it reached the island and went on downstream.

Tomorrow, maybe, there'd be warm sunshine, and we could go down to the old sycamore tree at the mouth of the cave, take the path through the swamp, and look all along the creek there for the boat.

"We'll make a new scarecrow!" Big Jim consoled Dragonfly—or tried to—but the little guy seemed all confused in his mind. His answer was, "He's getting sop-soaking-wet, and I never used to let him stay out in the rain."

Big Jim's voice got surly then, as he said, "Look, Roy! There isn't any *real* Snatzerpazooka anymore. He was just a make-believe playmate. Remember?"

In the kind of shadowy dark of the bridge, Dragonfly gave Big Jim a vacant stare, quick looked away down the creek toward the boat, and let out a yell that was almost a bloodcurdling scream. "*Look!* It's drifting across the creek!"

His excitement was contagious, like chicken pox. I felt goose bumps all over me as I looked through the blinding sheets of rain blowing over the rough water.

Had the wind changed? I wondered. Was it

now blowing from our side of the creek and pushing the boat *across* as well as *down*stream?

Dragonfly was right. The boat, which had been nearer our side when it passed under the bridge, now was on the other side of the middle and moving as fast toward the other shore as it was downstream. Faster, in fact.

I didn't even get a chance to think, *What on earth?*

The boat swung around a little, and I saw a hand clutching the gunwale. For a moment, I also saw something in the water that looked like a head-sized rubber ball.

I felt Dragonfly, beside me, clutching my arm with trembling hands. A second later he whispered, "It's a ghost. Snatzerpazooka's turned into a ghost! He's turning the boat around. He–he–he–look!" He screamed. "He's moving! He's waving his arm! The one that's been hanging over the edge!"

I really felt goose bumps then, because I'd seen it with my own eyes. The stuffed-with-straw right arm of Snatzerpazooka Scarecrow Gilbert *had* moved! And not as if it had been accidentally unbalanced but straight up in the air. Then it dropped down inside.

The boat began a faster drifting toward the other shore and almost disappeared behind an overhanging willow. Only the stern was visible, projecting about a foot beyond the end of the willow, with Snatzerpazooka's ridiculous head resting on the seat.

It was a tense minute, I tell you, and *spooky.*

How, I wondered, had the boat managed to drift *across* the creek? And how could it have steered itself, prow first, to the very place where, quite often, we ourselves tied it to a small maple at the water's edge? *How?*

Somebody had to do the steering. And *somebody* had to make it go faster than the wind and the current could have done it!

Right that second there was a blinding flash of lightning and a deafening crash of thunder at the same time, lighting up everything all around us and the area about the boat and the overhanging willow. At the same instant, I saw the lightning bolt, like a white-hot ball of fire, roar out of the sky and streak toward the old cottonwood tree over there. There was the sound of splitting wood, and, in the second before the lightning's light was gone, I saw a new white gash in the tree's trunk from a place about thirty feet up all the way to the ground.

I was scared for two reasons; first, because lightning so close with thunder that loud would scare anybody; and second, because I'd seen something else over there besides the boat with the scarecrow in it. I'd seen a human being clambering up the low embankment from the water's edge and hurrying toward the tree.

My mind's eye was seeing things, too: seven horses lying sprawled on each other under a lightning-struck sugar tree. And away over by itself, as dead as the seven other horses, lay a beautiful yellow and black and white pinto pony.

Now I knew for sure that there had been somebody swimming in the water, his body under and his head hidden behind the boat. He had been guiding the boat, pulling it along, making it go where he wanted it to. And I thought I knew who it was. The ball I'd thought I saw had been the red-haired head of Little Tom Till! It *had* to be Tom!

And then I could picture him over there, not more than fifteen feet from the shore, lying dead under the cottonwood tree.

I let out a nerve-tingling scream and yelled, *"It's Tom Till! He's been killed by lightning!"*

I shot headfirst out of our shelter under the bridge and scooted up the embankment into the driving rain, feeling it beating against my bare head and into my face.

I forgot about riding a big white stallion as my bare feet carried me across the board bridge to the other side. It was one of the wildest runs I'd ever made. I was hardly able to see because of the rain in my face.

"Tom! Tom! Tom!" I kept sobbing. *"Little Tom Till!"*

It seemed there wasn't anybody in the world I liked better right then. A lot of things about Tom went through my mind from the time I'd first met him in the Battle of Bumblebee Hill to the different experiences we'd had with him that very afternoon. I remembered his darting from behind the bushes at the bayou, gunnysack in hand, chasing the crippled crow. I saw the worried look in his eyes and his very scared look when he had started on that race to keep me from getting him.

I remembered the time I'd taken the cake over for his mother's birthday and I had yelled savagely at him, *"The very next time I catch you alone somewhere without Shorty or your brother along, I'm going to whale the living daylights out of you!"*

I'd said *that* to a boy who was one of my best friends! I'd said it to him and *meant* it!

And now, if Tom was dead, I'd never get a chance to be his friend again!

Run . . . run . . . pant . . . pant . . . the rain in my face, my bare feet pounding the board floor of the bridge . . . the thunder rumbling around in the sky . . . the wind whamming into me . . . *and a tornado in my mind!*

Across the bridge at last, down the embankment there, stumbling along the same path I'd run on that other time when I'd ruled my spirit enough to put out the brushfire with my red-and-green plaid shirt.

I had on that same red-and-green shirt right now, I thought.

Maybe Tom would still be alive when I got to him. He would not want to die, and maybe he would stagger away from the tree a little, the way Thunderball had done before he'd had to give up.

Now I was where the boat had put in to the shore. Now I was at the cottonwood, but I could hardly see the long, ugly, white gash on it. In spite of the rain, I *could* see well enough that Tom himself wasn't there anywhere.

Maybe he'd managed to get quite a few feet away. Maybe . . .

I worked myself around through the bushes, then stumbled over something and took a headfirst spill. I landed right in front of something dark and shaped like a triangle at the top. I couldn't stop myself from rolling and came to inside a low canvas room.

I had stumbled over Shorty and Tom's tent rope a few inches from where it was tied to a stake in the ground, had fallen headlong, rolled toward the canvas door, and struck it hard enough to force it open.

The black sky outside made it so dark inside that I could hardly see the cot against one wall. Directly across from it was another cot the same size, with something lying on it, not moving.

The rain on the canvas roof was so deafening I could hardly hear myself as I cried toward the prostrate form on the cot, "Tom! *Is that you?* Are you all right?"

There wasn't any answer, not even a groan.

Now I was beside him, my heart pounding and also my head where I'd struck it on the root.

"Tom!" I cried again. "Are you all right? Are you—"

Still there wasn't any answer.

My hands reached out to the form on the cot, felt it.

But it wasn't Tom. It wasn't anybody. It was only a pile of bedding. Tom wasn't there.

Where on earth was he?

And then I heard a groan from somewhere. The very second I heard it, I knew it was Tom Till's groan, and I knew where he was. He was *under* the cot, hiding.

I was on my hands and knees in the half-dark now, calling above the din on the roof, "Tom! Are you all right? Did you get struck by lightning?"

I reached under to touch him, but he shrank back farther under.

"Don't hurt me! Don't hurt me! I didn't mean to throw water in your face! I'm sorry!"

Just then I heard others of the gang coming. Before they would get there, I knew I had to say something to Tom. In my memory I was seeing myself standing by their picket gate and Tom by their wooden-handled pump. I seemed to feel again the splashing of cold well water in my face and hear Tom saying that only sissies went to Sunday school.

And just outside the gate was savage-faced Shorty Long with a baseball bat in his hands.

And again I was remembering I had said to Tom, "If I ever catch you alone somewhere . . . I'll whale the living daylights out of you."

Now I knew why Tom had run away from me. Why, even now, he was scared and begging me not to hurt him. Tom Till knew Bill Collins had a fierce temper when he wasn't ruling it, and he was afraid of me.

A big lump came up into my throat, and I exclaimed under the cot to him, "Come on out, Tom. I won't hurt you. I'm your friend. I want to be your friend, and I'm not mad at you anymore!"

It was one of the happiest endings to one of the most worried experiences of my life.

Tom hadn't any sooner believed me and come out, than the gang, wet as drowned kittens, came crawling into the tent. In a little while we had all explained everything to each other—almost everything, that is.

We were so happy that Tom was alive and all right that there wasn't a one of us who wasn't ready to forgive him for being Shorty Long's friend and acting ornery to us.

It was a wonderful feeling with everybody forgiven by everybody and nobody mad at anybody.

In about seven minutes the rain let up. In fact, all of a sudden it just stopped, and we all came out into the clean-smelling, storm-washed world and stretched our very wet selves and looked around to see what damage the storm had done.

That's when I exclaimed to Tom, "Hey! You had your tent pitched over *there*—how come it's here under the ponderosa? I thought—"

"We moved it that day you got stuck in the sycamore tree. Remember—you told us that about lightning!"

Then did I ever feel fine! *So* fine I could

have screamed to let out some of the happiness inside. The reason Tom Till was alive now instead of lying like a dead horse was because I'd ruled my spirit enough to tell even Shorty Long his tent was pitched in a dangerous place. I might not be better than any conqueror who captured a city, but I'll bet I *felt* better.

While we were looking at the ugly gash on the cottonwood's trunk, I noticed something else. On the ground, buried *in* the ground in the exact spot where the tent had been pitched before, was a big ten-inch-in-diameter branch that had fallen, broken off by the fierce wind.

I stood looking down at it, thinking, *Even if the lightning hadn't struck the tree, if Tom had been inside the tent under the cot, if the tent had been here instead of under the pine tree, he would have been killed by the falling branch.*

Just then, Dragonfly let out a happy yell, "Here comes old Redskin!"

I'd been in so much excitement that I hadn't even missed Dragonfly's grown-up puppy that had bloodhound blood in him.

We looked, and sure enough there was his dog, out in the middle of the creek, swimming as fast as he could to get across to where we were.

"Where's he been?" I asked.

"He's scared of storms. He always runs and hides when it thunders and lightnings."

There was one thing more that needed explaining. How had our scarecrow gotten into the boat? Somebody had to *put* it in.

Tom didn't want to tell us at first, until we promised we wouldn't hold it against him.

"Bob did it. But don't be mad at him. He's my brother. He threw it into the boat and shoved the boat out into the creek. I swam out to stop the boat from floating away. I heard you coming and got scared and . . ."

Tom looked at me, and I looked at him and grinned. He grinned back, and I knew for sure that we were friends again.

Just then Little Jim cried happily, "The sun's out! And there's a rainbow!"

And there *was* a rainbow, as pretty and bright as I'd ever seen. It was arched clear across the eastern sky. It was so extrabeautiful it almost hurt your heart to look at it.

My mind picked me up and took me in a flash back to the Collins living room just after the last electrical storm. I saw my mother standing, looking out the east window and saying reverently, *"I set My bow in the cloud."*

My thoughts were interrupted almost right away by Dragonfly letting out a long-tailed sneeze, followed by another and then another. Each sneeze had "Snatzerpazooka" mixed up in it, and that reminded us of our scarecrow.

We all went over to our boat and looked down at the saddest-looking thing you ever saw.

"Tomorrow, we'll come and get him and hang him up again," Big Jim said. "We'd all better be getting on home now, or our folks'll be worried half sick."

"*My* mother will," Dragonfly said. He hissed

to his dog and started on the run for the bridge. Then he stopped, looked back, and called to us, "We start for the Rockies the second week in July, if any of you want to go with us."

As I followed in the path, it seemed I was already on my way out West. In fact, all of a sudden I was a Western marshal on a beautiful white stallion, galloping across the plains through the sagebrush and the tumbleweed and shooting my six-shooters into the air to let everybody know that the law was on its way.

Moody Press, a ministry of the Moody Bible Institute,
is designed for education, evangelization, and edification.
If we may assist you in knowing more about Christ
and the Christian life, please write us without obligation:
Moody Press, c/o MLM, Chicago, IL 60610.